MW01230111

SADDLEBAG DISPATCHES MAGAZINE PRESENTS

LUNGERS, LAWDOGS, AND LEGENDS

BOOMTOWN TALES OF SILVER AND BLOOD

Saddlebag Dispatches, LCC
A Subsidiary of Oghma Communications
Bentonville, Arkansas
www.saddlebagdispatches.com

Lungers, Lawdogs & Legends: Boomtown Tales of Silver and Blood
Description: First Edition | Bentonville: Saddlebag Dispatches, 2024
Identifiers: ISBN: 978-1-63373-962-8 (trade paperback)| ISBN: 978-1-63373-963-5 (eBook)
FICTION/Westerns | FICTION/Action & Adventure |
FICTION/Thrillers/Historical

Trade Paperback edition August, 2024

Cover Design and Interior Design by Casey W. Cowan
Front Cover: *Return From the Hunt* by Frank Tenney Johnson (1874-1939)
Back Cover: *Estes Park, Long's Peak* by Albert Bierstadt (1830-1902)
Editing by Anthony Wood, Dennis Doty & Staci Troilo

SADDLEBAG DISPATCHES MAGAZINE PRESENTS

LUNGERS, LAWDOGS, AND LEGENDS

BOOMTOWN TALES OF SILVER AND BLOOD

Pike's Peak by Albert Bierstadt

TABLE OF CONTENTS

The Lost Greenhorn by Alfred Jacob Miller

LIST OF ILLUSTRATIONS

The Parley by Frederic Remington

PREFACE

BOOMTOWN! The very sound excited the heart to beat quicker'n a hog leg slapped from a cowhide holster. From the headwaters of the Arkansas River in the Rocky Mountains, sprung a mining camp straight from the earth, where a person's life wasn't worth the price of a mining claim, and the price of a drink cost more than a day's scratchings from the earth. Boomtown! Where the smell of opportunity and tragedy wafted thick in the air, and the chance to get rich drew the worst and best of humankind. Welcome to *Lungers, Lawdogs, and Legends: Boomtown Tales of Silver and Blood,* a collection of short stories centered on the famed mining town, Leadville, Colorado.

Boomtown—where miners, engineers, and merchants chased-wealth, and claim jumpers, speculators, and swindlers lurked in every shadowy corner. Where lungers sought relief and law dogs chased bandits to make names for themselves. Where miners struggled to show color and colorful characters sought to peddle their fame. Where young boys looked up to their fathers, and the cultured looked down their noses at hardworking commoners. Leadville, where soiled doves plied their wares, and saloon girls offered endless entertainment. Where world-renown legend of the stage, Oscar Wilde, performed, and famed *pistolero* of mythical proportions, Doc Holliday, enjoyed his last gun-playover a five dollar bet. It all happened in Leadville. Boomtown—grows faster than a speeding bullet and drops just as quick when the strike plays out.

Pour yourself a good cup of coffee, settle back against a log by the campfire, and enjoy yarns spun by award-winning authors Sharon Frame Gay, J.D. Arnold, P.A. O'Neil, Corinne Joy Brown, Candace Simar, Kyleigh McCloud, Anthony Wood, and others who bring you stories of a boomtown called Leadville, and other tales of the Old West.

—Anthony Wood
Managing Editor, *Saddlebag Dispatches*
June 17, 2024

SADDLEBAG DISPATCHES MAGAZINE PRESENTS

LUNGERS, LAWDOGS, AND LEGENDS

BOOMTOWN TALES OF SILVER AND BLOOD

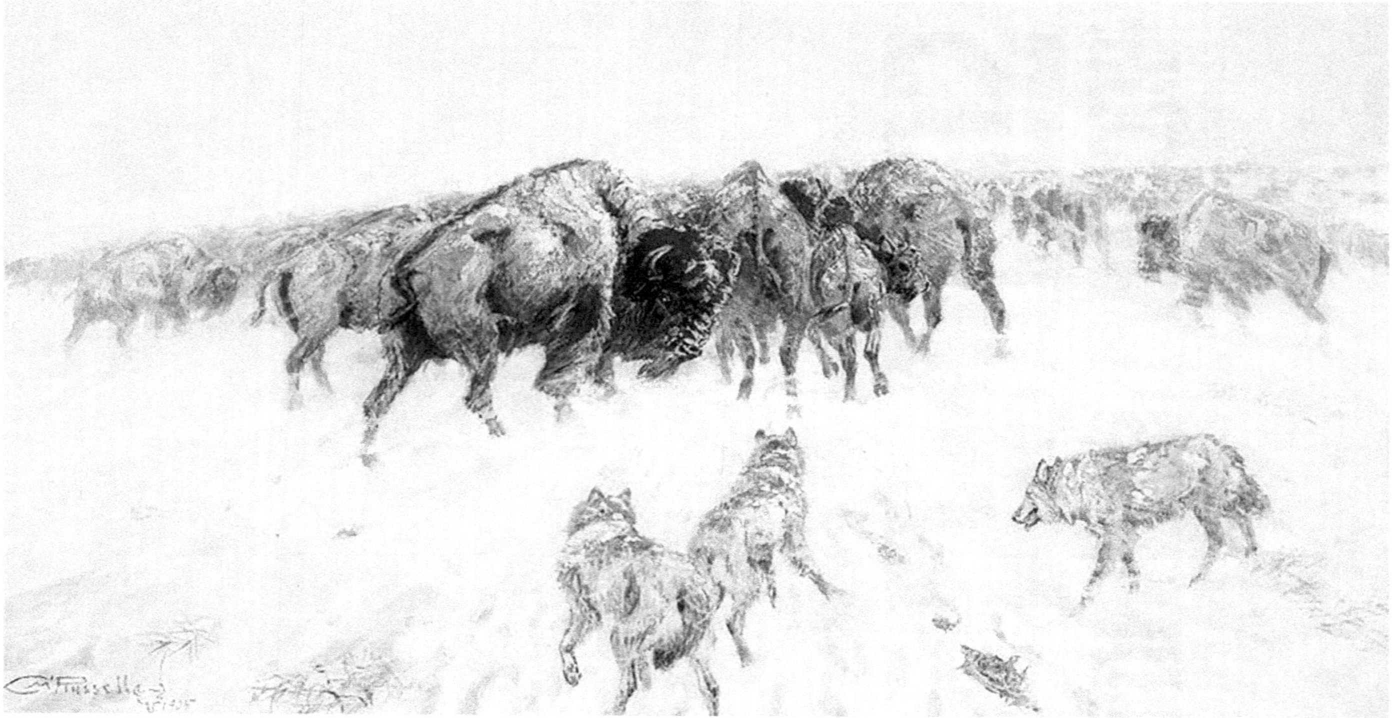

Montana Winter by Charles Marion Russell

HARD ROCK BOTTOM

WILL AMES

"GIMME A WHISKEY."

The barkeep didn't look up from scrubbing the rough cedar planks. "Not till I see the color of your money, Sam. We don't do credit anymore."

Sam's head snapped up and he scowled. "This ain't the day for games, Bud Ellis. Gimme a damn drink. You know I'm good for it."

Bud shook his head. "Sorry, Sam. No exceptions." He nodded at a stub of clapboard leaning in the corner with No Credit scrawled in charcoal, barely visible through the stale, sour smoke that hung thick under the low ceiling. "Nothing personal."

"Time was you were glad to get a single customer in this rat hole," Sam grumbled, digging in a pocket and wedging himself onto a wobbly stool between two other customers. He plunked a tiny, red-yellow nugget down on the bar. "There. Now gimme my damn drink."

Bud squinted at the nugget in the dim light. "That was before the boom and every two-bit prospector with a claim started promising to pay their tabs once they struck color," he said and pocketed the nugget. He turned over a dingy glass and nodded at the rough-bearded men in muddy denim drinking and playing cards at ramshackle tables. "I have a business to run. If I gave credit, I'd be out of liquor and business before you sourdoughs paid me a speck of color. Every one of you is just another spadeful away from striking it big." He poured two fingers and slid the drink to Sam, sloshing some as it bumped over the rough, knotty surface. "Or so y'all keep tellin' me."

"Just business, huh?" muttered Sam, sipping the whiskey. He grimaced and held it at arm's length, eyeballing it. "Jesus, Bud, what is this? I'd'a kept my gold if I'd known you were servin' kerosene now."

Bud shrugged. "Rye's all I got. Sign of the times." He took another grimy glass and set up the lanky man in a tweed suit to Sam's left. "Town's full to burstin'. I heard someone say we're pushin' ten thousand this year, if you can believe that, and all needin' supplies. The mule trains can't get here fast enough."

Sam forced the rye down and wiped his mouth. "Well, I see you're still chargin' for the good stuff," he grumbled, pushing the glass away.

"Be glad there's still whiskey to be had at all, friend," observed the thin man, wiping his short, square-clipped mustache. His face twisted up as he sipped, but he persevered, carefully clinking the glass down between droplets of spilled whiskey. "The last establishment I had the ill fortune to patronize served a sort of... homemade beverage. They, too, were short on necessities." He shook his head and pushed a pair of spectacles up his nose. "Believe me when I say rye is ambrosia in comparison." He tugged at his high, stiff collar and waved off a refill.

Bud grinned and shrugged again. "Sign of—"

"Sign of the times," muttered Sam, stuffing a battered, shapeless hat down over his bristly, white hair. "Yeah, yeah. I heard you the first time." He stood and nudged the spindly man, rolling his eyes. "Mark my words, Bud Ellis. I finally get through all that damned sand sludge and hit color, the first thing I'm gonna do is buy up that Golden Chalice joint across the street and put you out of business."

The thin man pushed his glass forward and stood as well, dabbing his mustache with a cream handkerchief. "An endeavor I support wholeheartedly, friend," he said.

"Just how is your claim coming, Sam?" asked Bud. "Figured you'd have struck paydirt weeks ago." He was polishing the thin man's glass, grinning. "I heard the Ma Deuce has been wheelin' it out by the cartload for two days now. Ain't they just next door to you?"

Sam flushed and stomped away through the smoke and noise and dirt.

HE HAD TO stop and wait for his eyes to adjust as he stepped into the street. He stood there, scratching himself, trying not to get run over by the herd of people milling around.

"Your friend has an annoyingly condescending manner."

Sam turned and squinted up at the thin man who'd reappeared at his shoulder and was straightening the sleeves of his black frock coat. The cuffs were beginning to fray, and he plucked a loose, black thread, frowning at it before tossing it away. Sam spat on the filthy, uneven walk that ran in front of the saloon and nodded. "Regular dictionary, ain't ya?" he asked the man.

"The benefits of a Harvard education, friend," the man said, twisting a bowler hat onto his head.

"Harvard, huh?" Sam patted his pockets. He was down to his last three nuggets. "That near Denver?"

The tall man laughed. "That's what I love about these boom towns. Such colorful people."

"Speakin' of color," muttered Sam, "I gotta see a man about a screen. Beg pardon." He nodded and turned away.

"Excuse me," said the man. "But did I hear you tell the proprietor about some sort of trouble with tar-like sand?"

Sam turned, scowling. "Damn stuff is like mud. Can't hardly work my claim because it keeps gummin' up the sluices." He jerked his thumb at the bustling streets. "That's the only reason I'm in this dump. A load of sand blew out my screen and now I'm outta action till I get some more."

The stranger's dark, sharp eyebrows furrowed. He pulled off his spectacles and polished them with his handkerchief. "Curious," he muttered. "Would you mind terribly if I inspected your workings, Mister… ah, regrettably, I did not catch your surname."

"Barlow." Sam squinted up at the man. "Why you wanna inspect my diggins', Harvard?"

The man smiled. "So colorful," he muttered, perching the spectacles back on his hooked nose. "Mister Barlow, one of the many fields I studied in Harvard was geology, and I believe I may be able to shed some light on your viscous sand problem."

"Well hot damn." said Sam. "Why didn't you lead with that? That's the best news I heard all week." He clapped the man on the back, staggering him. "You show me how to get my gold and I'll cut you in fifty-fifty. I ain't greedy."

Harvard smiled and tipped his bowler. "Most generous of you, but it's really not necessary. I have my own means, you see. I merely wish to see the West before I return to my inheritance."

Sam eyed his clothes. "Well, you might wanna get that inheritance soon so's you can get yourself a new fancy suit. That one looks a mite wore out."

Harvard frowned and picked at another thread. "Indeed. One of the many quirks of frontier travel, I'm afraid." He spread his hands. "Unfortunately, I've outpaced my baggage. I last saw it somewhere around... Bent's Fort, was it? I was hoping it would find me sooner rather than later. I find I miss a fresh change of clothes."

"Yeah, yeah." Sam waved a hand, already turning. "Listen, I gotta go find us that screen. You run on out to the claim and do your inspectin' or whatever and I'll be back soon as I can."

"Wait! How do I find your operation?" Harvard called.

"Can't miss it," called Sam. "East side of the gulch. Looks like a tinker's nightmare." And then he was swallowed by the crowd.

A HALF HOUR and another nugget later, he fought his way out of town, a roll of screen over one shoulder, and joined the winding line of squealing buckboards and people that stretched from Oro City to the far end of California Gulch. Even a mile away, the towering maze of sluices that shattered the skyline at crazy angles was visible. The gulch rang with hammerblows, scraping saws, and the rattle of rocks on sluiceboards, all muted by the shouting, cursing, laughing men working their claims.

He found Harvard already at his workings, bowler hat and coat gone, white sleeves rolled up beyond his elbows, digging through the muddy, brown leavings of one on Sam's dump sites.

"Jesus, Harvard, you don't waste time, do you?" said Sam, dumping the screen on the ground.

Harvard rose and pushed his spectacles up with a grimy hand. "Fascinating. Simply fascinating." He smiled and wiped his hands. "How long have you been dealing with your sand problem?" he asked.

"Ever since the get-go," Sam said. "For every ounce of color I get, I gotta sift through a wagonload of the damn stuff. It's thick as pine tar." Gravel crunched as he nudged the roll of screen with the toe of his boot. "This'll be my third roll in a month. Any more blowouts without paydirt and I'm sunk."

Harvard was digging through his pockets. "The sand builds up at the bottom of your sluice box, ruining your screen and, therefore, your filtering capabilities?"

"Yeah," Sam grumbled, rolling out the mesh. "None of the other outfits have half the trouble with the stuff. Been pullin' steady color for months, damn their luck." He nodded at the acres of sluiceboxes that zigzagged across the streambed. Hundreds of men swarmed across the claims, working the sluices, hauling buckets of water or wheelbarrows of sand and gravel, while others worked on the boxes themselves, mending the troughs or building new lines that ran down the slopes to the streambed below.

Harvard produced a jeweler's eyepiece and bent over a heap of tan sand, scooping some into his palm and shifting it back and forth with a thumb. "I might not be so quick to judge, Mister Barlow."

"What's that?" Sam looked up from tacking a length of screen over the mouth of a sluice.

"Have you ever heard of Cerussite, Mister Barlow?" Harvard asked, still squinting through the eyepiece.

"Ceru-*what?*"

"Cerussite." Harvard lowered the eyepiece. "Some call it lead-spar, or maybe white lead ore?"

"Oh." Sam grimaced and waved a hand. He bent back over the mesh, grunting as he stretched it tight and began sinking nails with solid thunks of his hammer. "Lead ain't worth much out here, Mister. Come sundown, you get a whole bunch of it flyin' around once the boys get a few barrels of Bud Ellis's panther piss in 'em. Hell, some smartass even started a petition to change the name from Oro City to Leadville."

Harvard smiled. "Yes, well, Cerussite is only part of what I found."

Sam stood up, swaying a little as the blood left his head. "Spit it out, Harvard. Either you got somethin' to say or you don't. Otherwise, I got diggin' to get to."

The smile widened. "Silver, Mister Barlow. Silver is what I found."

Sam blinked. "Silver? In brown sand?"

Harvard held his hand out, along with the jeweler's eye. "See for yourself. You might like an assay done to confirm my assessment, but I can almost guarantee those tiny flakes mixed with the sand are silver."

Sam peered at the sand, not bothering with the eyepiece. "I'll be damned." He looked at Harvard. "No joke?"

"No joke, Mister Barlow." He tapped his head. "Harvard education, remember?"

Sam nodded at the scattered piles of rubble dotting the riverbank. "I'll be damned. I've tossed out acres of the stuff chasin' gold."

"Well, I'd say your luck might be changing." Harvard pocketed the eyepiece. "Of course, there's still the problem of locating the vein. Silver is rarely found in placer deposits, and as you can see these particles are hardly worth your trouble." He tossed the sand away and pulled his handkerchief from a vest pocket to wipe his hands. "I fear this might call for hard rock mining practices."

"Hard rock nothin'," said Sam, slinging away his hammer. He grabbed Harvard's arm, knocking the handkerchief to the mud. "You know what this means?"

"Certainly." Harvard grimaced as the handkerchief disappeared under Sam's grimy, tattered brogans. "You are not, ah, sunk, as you so quaintly put it?"

"Sunk, hell. I'm rich!" Sam grabbed him in a bear hug. "All I gotta do is find the vein." He cackled and slapped Harvard's shoulder. "Dammit, boy, but that does it. I'm cuttin' you in!"

Harvard raised a finger, but Sam ignored him. "Don't interrupt me, sonny. I don't care if you're a king. You're gettin' a fair cut. Nobody ever called Sam Barlow a skinflint."

He grabbed Harvard's arm again and dug his last two gold nuggets from a pocket. "Now, lissen. Get over to Purcell's and get that assay done." He pushed the gold into Harvard's hand. "This should take care of it and then some. Give him both. Make damn sure he understands you were never there." He jerked a thumb at the hundreds of men working around them. "Word gets out this damn gulch has silver on top of gold, there'll be a second bonanza. It'll be standin' room only. Not to mention the claim-jumpin' scum that'll come after us."

"Claim jumping? I confess I'm not familiar with the term."

"Gutter trash," growled Sam. He jerked his chin at the men working around them. "Men too lazy to do an honest day's work like the rest of us. They wait till you strike color and then come after your claim. Sometimes at the point of a gun, or maybe cross-filin' on you with fake papers if they feel like playin' nice. 'Course, there's some old boys'd rather cut your throat on a dark night and dump you in the hills. Cut out the legalities, you might say...." He slid a thumb across his throat.

Harvard shuddered. "Surely the constabulary takes steps to prevent such measures?"

"Constable? Jesus, Harvard." Sam thrust a stubby finger at Oro City. "You go through town with your eyes closed or somethin'? Ain't a peace officer for near seventy mile. Just the week before you showed up we had three shot and one cut, all over claims. And that was a slow week."

Harvard shook his head. "Surely there must be some law. Otherwise, what's to stop wholesale bloodshed over the wealth being recovered here daily?"

Sam smiled. "Hold on, sonny. I said there weren't no peace officers. Didn't say nothin' about no law." He went over to the stout wheelbarrow sitting beside the sluices and pulled a cut down, double-barreled shotgun from beneath the bucket. "This here's Eudora," he grinned, patting the worn stock. "She keeps the peace on my claim." He waved the stubby barrels under Harvard's nose. "Ten gauge. Had her cut down special to sit a holster just the underside of that barrow."

Harvard leaned back from the twin bores and swallowed hard. "Very clever."

Sam grinned. "Little trick I learned back in '49." He stowed Eudora back under the barrow. "Out here a man's his own law, son. But there ain't no sense courting trouble if we don't have to. That's why we keep the assay quiet."

"Understood," nodded Harvard. He pulled off his spectacles and began polishing them on his kerchief. "So what will you be doing while I get the assay?"

Sam scratched his wooly neck. "Gettin' supplies. We're gonna need an augur and a shitload of powder and fuses."

"But what about your ah... lack of funds, if I may be so indelicate. I do seem to remember your barkeep friend said credit was becoming a rarity."

Sam waved a hand. "This here's a boom town, son. Fortunes are made and lost quicker'n a preacher's son in a whorehouse. There's always a way to get credit. You just gotta know how to ask." He smiled and nodded at the heaps of sand. "You just worry about that assay." He stuck out a gnarled hand. "Partner?"

Harvard looked at his own hand, covered in muck and grit. "Partner," he said, and they shook.

"YOU A SMOKIN' man, Harvard?"

Harvard patted his shirt pocket. "Snuff, actually. I find it refreshes the mind wonderfully. Would you like a snort?"

"Blue bloods," Sam muttered. He tugged a pair of long cigars from his jeans and handed one to Harvard. "The fat lady don't sing for snuff, son. She likes a man's habit, so clamp on and let's get this hooraw started."

Harvard rolled the cigar in long fingers and ran it under his nose, breathing deep, then bit off the end and spat the shred away, clamping the cigar in his jaws. He raised his eyebrow at Sam, and Sam grinned around his own cigar. "Now that's more like it." He struck a match and cupped it around his cigar, it's flickering light making shadows in the deep lines of his face, and then lit Harvard's. A few puffs and dirty, fragrant smoke drifted up and was whisked away on the evening breeze. Sam blew a plume skywards and sighed. "That's better." He cocked an ear and looked sidelong at Harvard. "You hear that?"

Harvard frowned around the cigar. "Hear what?"

Sam grinned. "The ol' girl's singin'." He bent and fished a long fuse out of the dirt. "Now let's make her some music." He stuck the smoldering cigar to the fuse and held it tight until the hemp caught and more smoke started lazing upwards.

"Uh, Sam?"

"Eh?"

"Won't that make a lot of noise?"

"Bet your ass it will."

"What about keeping things quiet? Won't people be curious as to what we're up to?"

Sam shrugged as the burning fuse began to eat its way toward his hand. "You heard Bud Ellis. I been a runnin' joke ever since everyone else but me started pullin' color." He stared at the glowing cigar. More smoke plumed from his nostrils and he dropped the fuse just before the flame reached his fingers. "But that's about to change."

THE FIRST BLAST sent shards of rock zipping over their heads, some plinking off the sluices, others whistling into the darkening sky.

"She's singin' good now!" cackled Sam. He picked up Harvard from where he'd thrown himself flat in the mud and gravel and dusted him off. Harvard mouthed something, but Sam shook his head and wiggled a finger in his hairy ear. "Reckon I used a little too much powder?"

"Raving lunatic..." muttered Harvard, picking at the gritty muck staining his suit.

"Heh?"

"I said are you experienced in the use of those charges?"

Sam grinned. "Never touched the stuff before."

"Providence watch over us..."

Sam waved away puffs of smoke that drifted across their hiding spot behind a tall mound of waste rock. "Whew. Smells like rotten eggs, don't it. Hand me that shovel, will ya? We gotta clear away before we can blast again."

"What the hell was that?" called a voice from the gloom. Sam and Harvard looked up to see half a dozen rough-bearded men in filthy denim come in the lantern light and peer down into the smoking crater.

A short, bow-legged man elbowed his way to the front, swaying on the lip of the hole. He cocked his head at the night sky and squinted. "Someone shootin' a cannon at us?" he slurred, waving a half-empty bottle at the smoking crater.

"Those were mining charges, dolt," said the first man, pushing a grimy cap back on his forehead. He shoved the little man stumbling into a shoeless miner in tattered dungarees.

"Dammit, Del, watch where you're goin'," grumbled the shoeless man, pushing him back the other direction. "If'n you weren't too drunk to see past the end of that lump you call a nose, you'd see it's just ol' Sam and that dandy playin' with black powder." The others chuckled as Del caught himself at the edge of the pit and teetered there, swaying as he tried to keep his balance.

"What's the matter, Sam?" asked the man in the cap. He hooked a thumb in his waistband and grinned around a fat cigar. "Can't you find no color above ground?"

"The hell you want, Jenkins?" growled Sam.

Jenkins jerked a thumb at the darkness further up the gulch. "Came to see what all the fuss was about. Thought mebbe someone was gettin' his claim jumped." He grinned and waved the cigar at the hole. "Figured you'd'a' pulled up stakes months ago. Man can only take so much a'watchin' everyone around him get rich while he's workin' for pocket change." Even in the purpling dusk Sam's face was dark and flushed. "Tell you what, though," Jenkins continued. "I like your grit. You start seein' Chinamen t'other end of that hole, pack on up and come over to the Ma Deuce with us." Jenkins elbowed the shoeless man and grinned. "I'd trade ol' Del for a good mole any day." The others roared and slapped their thighs, doubled over with laughter.

Del, still swaying, leered at him and drained the rest of his bottle in one go. With a belch, he tossed it into the crater and pointed, giggling even as he teetered. Jenkins grabbed his collar and yanked him stumbling backwards. "Come on, you idiot, let's get outta here before you fall in and Ol' Sam blows you to kingdom come." The miners staggered away, cackling and swaying. "Keep it down, will ya' Sam?"

one called back. "Some of us are tryin' to take it easy." And then the gloom swallowed them up.

Harvard put his hand on Sam's arm. "Come on, Sam," he murmured. "We've work to do."

Sam resisted, eyes fixed on the gloom hiding the miners.

Harvard put a little weight into his pull. "Sam. Let them go. The silver?" He gave a shake and Sam's head finally snapped around. He glared at Harvard, the muscles in his neck taut. "Gimme that damn shovel," he said.

SAM DUMPED THE last spadeful into the bucket squatting in the middle of the pit and shuffled through the clinking shards by the light of the lantern. "Damn," he muttered, voice echoing off the jagged walls. He squinted at a large chunk and tossed it up to Harvard at the edge of the pit. "More damn lead." He stood and dusted off his denim. "Dammit, Harvard. I thought we'd done it. Slope a little, follow the lead-spar til it leads us to the silver. But we're two days deep and still pullin' lead by the bucketload. I'm startin' to wonder if we're ever gonna strike that ledge."

Harvard inspected the ore with his eyepiece. "You know, Sam, lead may not be flashy, but it is still a profitable mineral. As you said yourself, it is quite popular on the frontier."

Sam scowled up at him. "Son, you think I come this far with this much trouble to settle for lead, you got another thing comin'. Half measures are for quitters. Now get me an empty bucket. We got rock to move." He snagged a small, burlap sack of powder and a length of fuse from a pile in the corner and tucked them into his belt as he ducked into the low shaft. The lantern light shrank to a dull glow that barely lit the rubble-covered floor. "Mebbe I oughta up the powder a bit..." echoed his grumbling voice.

Harvard shook his head and stepped away from the pit. The chunk of ore bounced from hand to hand in time with his low whistling and he tossed it into a growing heap separate from the other piles. He toed through the ore, scribbling marks on a scrap of paper with a stubby pencil as the muffled crack of another powder charge echoed behind him. He made a few more marks, then nodded to himself, a small smile touching his face. With the lantern half-raised, he squinted left and right into the gloom.

"Be right back, Sam," he called. "I need the wheelbarrow to move this mountain of detritus you're attempting to bury us under."

"De-what?" Sam muttered. Metal scraped against rock, muffling more grumbling. "The hell does he think he's talkin' to?"

Harvard smiled and strode off, lantern high, whistling.

SAM STAGGERED OUT under a heavy shovelful and stopped when he saw the full bucket still sitting on the pit floor. "Dammit, Harvard!" he roared. "Where the hell are you? I thought you were clearin' this mess up?" The rickety ladder leaning against the wall creaked as his head popped above ground and he squinted into the gloom, lantern high. "Harvard?"

"Here, Mister Barlow."

Sam turned around and craned his neck up. Harvard stood on the opposite lip of the crater, Sam's stubby shotgun in his thin hands, lantern at his feet.

Sam squinted. "The hell you doin' with Eudora, Harvard?"

Harvard's eyes were black caverns in the lantern glow. "I believe you called it 'claim jumping'." A half smile touched one corner of his mouth. "I'm afraid our partnership has run its course, Sam."

Sam scowled. "I thought you didn't need no fortune, bein' a man of means and such."

Harvard shook his head. "I'm afraid that's only half the truth." He turned a fraying cuff to the lantern light and grimaced. "I am indeed a man of means. Or I was. I've developed a bit gambling habit, you see, and so my parents have disinherited me on the grounds of my..." he spread his arms and a sneer twisted his face, "profligate lifestyle..." He plucked at his worn suit, Eudora's twin muzzles waving in the gloom. "You and I are more alike than you think; ruined unless this claim bears fruit." Then the gaping, black bores lowered to center on Sam's chest as he re-steadied his grip. "But now that you've been bringing up quality ore for two days now, so I'm satisfied we're onto a truly rich strike."

"Two days? You mean I've been neck deep in silver for two whole days?" Sam scratched ragged whiskers and craned his neck over the rim to peer into the gloom. He nodded at the pile of mottled gray shards. "All that?"

"All that."

Sam shook his head. "Finally struck color... I'll be damned." He looked back at Harvard. "And now you're gonna take it from me. I trusted you."

Harvard grimaced. "I wish there were another way. I do. But you must understand my position."

"Understand your position..." muttered Sam. He raised his shovel. "I understand perfectly, you damn backstabbin'—"

"Now, now," Harvard jabbed Eudora at him. "That's quite enough of that. Put the shovel down before you do something rash."

Sam eyed him a heartbeat and then let out a breath. The shovel went clanging to the scree and he plopped down beside it. He pushed his tattered hat back and rested his hands on his knees. "So how's this gonna work? Shotgun blast makes a mess."

Harvard shrugged. "Black powder. You were tired, got careless. Simply another mining accident. And because you made me your partner, no one will think twice once I take over full ownership. A tidy coup, if I may."

Sam sighed. "Think you know someone..." He fished around in his shirt pocket and pulled out the stub of a cigar and a match. "Was savin' this for when we hit paydirt. Guess it don't matter now." He struck the match and puffed the cigar to life. Smoke plumed from his nostrils and he sighed again. "I'll say one thing for you, son. You're a slick sonofabitch, but damned if I don't like you. Damn shame to end it like this." Then he flicked the still burning match onto the gunny-sacks of powder and coiled fuse.

Harvard's eyes widened and he leapt back, but before he took two steps, Sam snatched the powder sack from his belt, lit the drawstring burlap with his cigar, and lobbed it at Harvard. It thumped down just behind him, and he yelped and stumbled back, but he tripped on loose ore and plunged into the pit where his shriek was cut off as he landed on Eudora.

In a heartbeat Sam was up and across the pit. Tiny flames had started on the excess bunched at the mouth of one sack and he scooped it up and tossed it deep into the shaft he'd dug and then hit the dirt as the ripping crack blasted smoke and tiny slivers of ore across the width of the pit, peppering his head and arms.

When the ringing finally stopped, he looked up. "Damn shame," he sighed.

"GIMME A WHISKEY."

"Now, Sam, you know the drill."

Sam glared. "Shut your damn mouth and pour, Bud Ellis."

Ellis eyed Sam for a heartbeat and then slid a drink down.

Sam tossed it back and plunked the glass down. "Another."

Ellis opened his mouth, hesitated, and then poured another. "Heard about the accident."

Sam killed the second and reached for another.

"Reckon you ought to take it easy?" Ellis asked. "You won't be worth a plugged nickel come tomorrow."

"I'm pullin' up stakes," Sam grunted. "Hit me again."

Ellis' eyes widened. "You're callin' it quits?" He shook his head. "I swear. Never thought I'd see the day."

Sam stared at the back wall. "Hit me again."

Ellis hesitated. "If you're hangin' it up…" he set the bottle down.

Sam snorted and tossed a red-yellow nugget on the counter. "Things never change, huh, Bud? All that matters is you get your money."

Ellis shrugged. "Just business, Sam. Got myself to look after."

"Well don't worry about your business," growled Sam. "I sold to some foreign feller with deep pockets. Now. Hit. Me. Again."

Bud Ellis poured as fast as Sam could drink.

"So what's next?" Ellis asked. "Hear the boys working California Gulch are pulling in good color."

"Nope," grunted Sam. He swayed where he sat, still looking at nothing. "I'm done prospectin'."

"Done? What about your gold?"

"Damn the gold." Sam tossed back a final shot and stood. "You can have it." Then he turned and stumbled outside.

—Despite being born and raised along the sunny shores of the Gulf Coast, Will Ames grew up dreaming of horses, six-guns, and wide, rolling prairies. Nearly every second not spent chasing fish up and down countless miles of beaches, bays, and lagoons was taken up by cattle drives and prairie schooners, war parties and weary cavalry patrols, both on screen and in print. Once he'd exhausted just about every classic Western story ever created, he thought the natural next step should be to create his own. And an aspiring author, he hopes he can reinvigorate the stories of the spirit that shaped our country and perhaps one day even earn a place on the shelf next to those legends who set the bar so very high. A proud and lifelong Alabamian, he nevertheless hopes to one day see firsthand the big sky country that has haunted his dreams.

THE GHOST OF LEADVILLE

SHARON FRAME GAY

LEADVILLE, COLORADO —1882

"HELL NO. ARE you crazy? I ain't gonna do that!" My best friend, Will Jenkins, pursed his lips and aimed toward the tin can five feet away. A stream of spit flew across the lot, missing the target by three feet. He shrugged. "Well, that's a start, anyway."

My buddy and I were learning how to spit like the miners. So far, the can remained untouched. We were both twelve years old that summer. Neither one of us could spit very far, but we had broad ambition and time on our hands.

School was out in Leadville. At first, we relished our freedom. But as the weeks marched by in this mining town with stingy air, the boyish glee of no classes lost its luster.

Besides, a lot of bad things happened around here, and dwelling on it made it worse.

Will's refusal to my question puzzled me. Here I was, offerin' him the adventure of a lifetime, and he flat out said no.

"Why not?" Now it was my chance at the can. The saliva landed pitifully on the tip of my boot.

Will grinned. "I win, Rob! You ain't got the spit of a man yet. Me, on the other hand, can hock like a cobra!"

"You didn't answer my question." I punched him in the arm.

Will glared at me. "You *know* why not! We've been told all our lives to stay out of those silver mines! We fall down a hole and nobody will find us until we've starved to death. If we even survive the fall! My Uncle Wallace tells me there are mine shafts all around this town and it isn't safe for kids to play around them. He said he and my dad would whop me until my trousers bled." Will worked up another wad of spit and sent it shooting against a rock. It slid along the surface to the ground. He grinned in satisfaction, then wiped his mouth with a ragged sleeve. "Why do you want to go down there, anyway?"

I shrugged. "I thought I might find a ghost. Missus Conroy says the place is full of 'haints', as she calls them. That means ghosts and demons and such. She says the mines in Ireland are full of 'em. Banshees haunt those mines, too."

"That sounds stupid. What good would it do to meet a ghost in the first place?"

I looked away so Will couldn't see me tear up. "Well, you know, I was hopin' to find my pa down there."

Will flinched. My father died in May from a mining accident. The mine boss told us he must have gone in there after the crew went home to fetch something, tripped and fell all the way to the bottom of the shaft. Nobody would let me look at him when they brought him out of the mine. I wanted to see him one last time, but I suppose it was for the best that I didn't.

I thought my mama was gonna die herself, right then and there that day. She folded to the ground like a jackknife, and no amount of comfort could make her stand upright for a long time. Me and my little sister, Jane, huddled behind her and wailed until I'm sure those Banshees over in Ireland heard it.

Since then, nothing's been the same. It seems like the sun just won't shine anymore. I do my best to help my mother and Jane, but I'm just a kid myself. When I go outside with my friends and we laugh and play, I feel guilty I'm not rolling in the dirt in agony all the time over my father's death. Then I come home flustered and angry and toss and turn at night. I look for answers and can't find 'em.

I kept thinking about old Mrs. Conroy and her story about the ghosts. The more I thought about it, the more I figured my father's ghost was somewhere in The Silver Wolf mine. Maybe Papa needed me as much as I needed him. Maybe he'd let me know everything was gonna be okay. He'd tell me I was just a kid, and my mother and Jane were gonna be fine, and I could go back to playing and spitting at tin cans. Then maybe I'd say it's okay for him to leave the mine and fly on up to heaven. We'll miss him, but we'll get by, and he can stop bein' a ghost and kneel at the foot of the Lord. Maybe he could tell God a thing or two about mining, or fill him in about us, down here on earth, and how life can be so beautiful, but so full of misery, too. Like the misery I feel in my heart every time I think of my father coming up from that mine shaft into the sunshine, dead as can be. They buried his poor body in the rocky Colorado soil, far away from our home in West Virginia, where we lived until Papa brought us here.

Will put his hand on my shoulder. "I'm sorry, Robbie. I'm sorry your daddy died. But I just can't bring myself to go down into that mine shaft, lookin' around for ghosts. I mean, what if we conjure up the wrong one, and it's an evil ghost, and it pokes out our eyes with his fingers and then we can't ever find our way outta there? I just can't. Besides, somebody would see us and make us leave."

"Not at night."

"At night? Are you crazy? Nobody goes into those tunnels at night! You can't see a thing!"

I snorted. "You can't see a thing in the daylight either, you dope. I'd bring one of my pa's lamps and I'll see plenty good."

By now, I'd warmed to the subject and convinced myself it was something I had to do. I stood up and dusted off my pants. Then spit clear across to the tin. It hit with a tiny ping. I puffed out my chest and looked down at Will.

"If you ain't coming with me, I'll go alone."

"Suit yourself." Will shrugged and tossed a pebble at the can, then we wandered home and talked no more about the mine. He probably figured I'd given up. But he was wrong. I didn't talk about it because I was gonna do it.

It seemed like dinner stretched on for hours that night. I wolfed down my food and jumped up from the table before Mama and Jane finished eating.

"If you're done, feed Rosie," Mama said.

Rosie the canary paced on her perch in the small wooden cage my father had built. He kept Rosie like other miners do, taking a bird or a mouse down into the shaft to make sure there was air to breathe. If the air was too thin, the canary could die. Rosie never got woozy in the mine. Now that Papa is dead, she won't have to find out what it's like not to breathe, like my father found out.

I tossed some seeds to Rosie, then yawned and stretched my arms. My mother looked up from her plate.

"You tired, Robbie?"

"Sure am. Will and I played hard today." I sidled towards the bedroom and nudged Frankie, our dog, out of the way with my foot. "Guess I'll turn in early."

I stepped into my room and closed the door. I'd already hid one of Papa's miner lamps under the bed. A handful of matches sat on my dresser like an accusation. Next to it was a red coat my father bought me at the mercantile before he died. It was the last thing he ever gave me. I planned on wearing it, to show him how much I love it and how much I love him. I wanted to cry just thinking about it. Maybe he'd wrap his arm around my neck like he used to and draw me into him. I imagined him planting a kiss on the top of my head and tellin' me I was the best son a man could ask for.

I unlatched the window and pushed on the pane. It groaned and swung out into the night air. Throwing myself on the bed, I lay there for what seemed like hours, watching the stars wheel across the sky, waiting for the house to grow still.

I must have fallen asleep because the next time I opened my eyes, it was the middle of the night. A coyote in the distance let loose with a mournful howl. I bolted out of bed and pulled on my clothes, grabbed the matches and lamp, then slipped out the window easy as pie. Part of me wished Mama heard and called me back in, but I had to see if Papa was in that mine, so I could set his ghost free.

The Silver Wolf wasn't too far out of town. A well-trod trail led past the outskirts of Leadville and up into the hills. I heard a coyote singin' out in the distance again and thought maybe Will was right. This was a crazy idea.

The mine loomed above the trail as it widened. In front of the entrance were ore cars and debris. Rocks and dirt formed small hills on both sides of the opening. Huge timbers supported the entrance with a sign that said "The Silver Wolf". Creeping closer, I smelled a dank, earthy odor coming from the gaping hole in the hillside.

I only hesitated a moment. Then I lit the lamp and marched right into The Silver Wolf like I wasn't scared at all, even though my heart pounded so loud I figured the whole town of Leadville could hear it. Wading into the shadows, I swept the light in front of me, a step at a time. A dark tunnel wound off to my right. On the left was a wide stretch that seemed to lead nowhere. So, I placed a foot into the tunnel and waved the lamp. A colony of bats fluttered over my head, causing a ruckus. I ducked and held my breath. Then, all was quiet. An eerie quiet. The kind of quiet like somebody might be holding their breath, too.

The passage continued downward, and I followed it. Along the wall were several ore cars, some with rocks and dirt in them, some empty. Ahead was a bend in the tunnel. I squeezed my eyes and tried to commit to memory where I was so I could go back. A person could get lost in here, and many folks have. Right then and there, I figured I wouldn't need to travel too far to conjure up my father. He'd recognize my voice wherever his soul was sittin' in this mine and come to me.

I swung the lamp in front of my face so he could see me real good. "Papa?" I whispered. I listened for a while, then cleared my throat and called out again. But softly, remembering Will sayin' maybe another ghost might come instead. An evil one.

Just then, a gust of air from the shaft blew out the light. I shivered and strained to see in the gloom.

"Papa? Are you here?"

A voice rang out behind me. I just about jumped outta my skin.

Papa!

I was about to answer when the voice grew louder.

"So, why are we here, Payton?"

"We have to talk. I figured this place was best, so nobody will overhear us."

I recognized the first voice as James O'Malley, the mine boss. His Irish lilt echoed along the shaft. It was musical and yet serious, the way a preacher might read you the gospel in a friendly way, only he's really lettin' you know you're going straight to hell.

Then the two men argued. Their voices rocked back and forth, angry and loud. Curious, I edged closer.

"O'Malley," the other man said, "I know what the hell you've been doin' and it stops here and now."

"I don't know what you're talking about."

"Yes, you do! You're skimmin' off the owners of The Silver Wolf, and you stole the extra money they gave you for better safety measures, too. We're all suffering, no thanks to you. Why, just three months ago we lost Robert Steen."

Robert Steen? My father! I crept closer, stood on tip-toe and craned my neck around the corner to see them. I knew Mr. O'Malley, but the other man was a stranger. In the shimmering beams of their lamps, they took on a spooky look. The light wavered around their faces, while their lower bodies and legs were hidden in darkness. They looked like two angry heads, just floatin' in the mine, hollering at each other.

"You're a liar, Payton, and ain't nobody gonna listen to you, anyway. I can't have such disloyalty here at The Silver Wolf. You're fired!"

"Fired! Why, you son of a bitch! You're stealing from the company and you have the nerve to fire me? I'm here tonight to tell you to get out of town. Leave now, and nobody will be the wiser about what you did. Steen and I saw your books. We saw the cheatin'. What else have you done, O'Malley?"

"What do you mean?"

"I mean, it was mighty convenient that Robert died, wasn't it? Was it an accident? Or did you push him? I'm warning you. Get out of Leadville. I won't tell on you if you go tonight."

"Oh yeah, and what's in it for you?"

Silence. Then, "I figure you can give me a few thousand dollars. If you do, I'll turn away and you can walk out of here a free man. If you don't, I'm getting' Sheriff Johnson in on this, and you'll be going to jail."

Mr. O'Malley laughed. "Now, that's a hoot! The sheriff and I have an understanding. He's been on the dole for years. There aint' nobody gonna finger me here in Leadville, not even you, Payton."

My foot slipped on a pebble, and it rolled down the passage. O'Malley jerked his head and looked my way. I ducked back behind the wall. That's when Payton must have jumped him, because there was a scuffle. The two men were grunting and swearing. The mine echoed with their voices.

Then I heard a sickening sound, and a sigh, followed by silence.

I peeked around the corner again. O'Malley was towering above the other man with a pickaxe in his hand. Blood gushed from Payton's skull and soaked into the dirt floor.

Backing away, I knew I couldn't run anywhere but down into the tunnel. I felt my way in the gloom past an ore car and felt inside. It was full of rocks and soil. The next one was empty, so I struggled into the car, then lay flat on the bottom, looking up at the low ceiling.

The tunnel burst with light as O'Malley came my way. His breathing was heavy, as though he were dragging the other man behind him. As he grew closer, I feared he'd put Payton in the ore car where I hid. My heart thudded. I held my breath as he drew alongside me. He paused for a moment, then continued on.

I drew myself up and peered over the edge. O'Malley had Payton by the feet and tugged him along the passage. Ahead was the corner I was afraid to turn down earlier. I watched the boss disappear into the darkness. After a while, the sound of a shovel rang out in a rhythmic sound.

That's when I crawled out of the car and headed towards the entrance, my hands feeling along the wall in the dark. A bat brushed against my head, stirring my hair in its frenzy. Flailing my arms, I tripped and fell to my knees.

"Hey, who's there?" O'Malley shouted behind me. "Come back here!"

O'Malley's lantern lit up the tunnel as I stumbled through the passage. The heavy tread of his boots grew closer as I raced towards the entrance.

I bolted out of the mine past the ore cars, jumped between them, then climbed towards the top of the hill.

A bullet whizzed past my ear. I yelped. Another bullet spit into the dirt on my right, then on my left. Dodging between trees and rocks, I disappeared into the night.

Praying not to fall into a mine shaft, I picked my way deep into the hills for hours, then crept back into Leadville before dawn, peering over my shoulder in terror.

O'Malley would be after me. There was no doubt about that. He probably didn't recognize who I was from the back, but my red coat probably stuck out like a sore thumb. All he had to do was look around Leadville for a kid in that coat. Terrified, I tore it off and let it fall to the ground. I sobbed as I stumbled home.

My mind turned cartwheels. What was I to do? He told Payton about his deal with the sheriff, so I knew I couldn't go to the law for help. I pictured O'Malley coming to my house, killing me, Mama, and Jane. But if he didn't see my face, would he know it was me?

The house was quiet as I dove back through the window, latched it, and huddled against the wall. I felt like the loneliest boy in the world. Nobody to talk to, nobody to help me figure this out. Sometime before dawn, I fell asleep on the floor and didn't wake until late morning.

The best idea, I decided, was to do nothing and see what might happen. Maybe he'd forget about it. Very unlikely, I thought, but maybe I'd have time to come up with a plan.

For two days, I hung around the house. Mama asked me if I was feelin' sick because I didn't go out, not even when Will came by and knocked on my window, holding up the tin can. I shook my head and gave him the stink-eye. He shrugged and walked away.

From the living room window, I could see up and down Harrison Avenue. People bustled back and forth, from one side to another, like ants on a hillside. Horses and wagons drifted by, miners walked to work, children played in the street with hoops.

O'Malley wandered up and down the avenue, peering into windows and staring long at the children as he walked by.

Last night, word traveled that Bill Payton didn't show up for work at The Silver Wolf. His wife and children were frantic. Several men formed a search party, but came up with nothing. I figured O'Malley buried him in a secret spot.

On the third day, as I continued my vigil at the window, I was shocked to see a boy about my age wearing my red coat. He must have found it! If O'Malley saw it, he'd kill that kid for sure! I planted my face in my hands and moaned. Now I'd done it. I might as well just kill that boy myself. It was all my fault. I should have listened to Will and never gone looking for my father.

There was only one answer. I had to get that coat back from him and save at least one life. I searched for O'Malley or the sheriff as I eased out the door and into the street. All was quiet. The red coat turned down an alley, and I followed. The boy knelt down to pick up a rock and put it in his pocket as I hurried to catch up.

"Hey there, wait!" I shouted.

The boy stopped and turned around. He was older than me. Bigger, too. The jacket didn't even come down to his wrists and rode high above his waist. I didn't know who he was.

I approached slowly.

"Whaddya want?" He glared at me with green eyes that floated in a face full of freckles.

"That's my jacket you got there. I lost it a few days back." I glanced down the alley to make sure we weren't followed and held out my hand. "Give it back."

He narrowed his gaze and laughed. "It belongs to me now, kid. Get the hell outta here!"

"You can't have it! My father gave it to me! Hand it over!"

"Shut up! I ain't givin' it to you. Get outta here!"

He shoved me backwards, and I fell to the ground. Then he tugged the rock out of his pocket and hit me square in the chin with it.

I winced and felt around for a rock to throw back at him, but he'd already turned and raced down the alley, then disappeared.

I sat in the dirt and rubbed my bleeding chin. Not only did I know who killed my father and Bill Payton, but I figured this kid was gonna get killed, too. There was no hope. Nowhere to go, nobody to tell.

Then, just as plain as day, I heard my father's voice in my head, just like he was whisperin' in my ear.

"Robbie, go see Old Man Flanagan who lives down by the churchyard. He'll help you."

I knew Mr. Flanagan, but not well. Sometimes after church, my father stopped to talk to him. He lived in a tiny shack behind the cemetery. Flanagan was an old gold miner who never struck it rich. Now he was too ancient and crippled to mine, and my papa brought him ham hocks and bags of flour and tobacco sometimes. They'd sit and talk about the old days in Leadville.

I sneaked out of the alley and high-tailed it over to the churchyard. The old shack wasn't hard to find. Old Man Flanagan was sittin' on a stoop, whittling a piece of wood. He looked up as I approached, one eye cloudy lookin', the other sharp as an eagle.

"Well, who's this comin' to see me?" He glared at me with his good eye, and I felt like maybe this wasn't a good idea. Hell, maybe he was in cahoots with the sheriff and O'Malley.

"Speak up, boy! I ain't got time to have you stand there and gawk at me."

"I'm Robbie Steen," I spoke around a lump in my throat.

"Robert's boy?" He straightened, set the knife down, and dusted the shavings off his lap. "Sorry to hear about your daddy, son. He was a good man."

I nodded. "Thank you, Mister Flanagan."

"So, Robbie, what's on your mind?"

I hesitated. Took a step back. Wrung my hands. Sweat broke out on my forehead.

"Hey, hey, son. It's okay. Don't spook. Whatever it is, maybe I can help." He held out a calloused hand and beckoned me closer.

That's all it took. I needed a grown-up. I needed a friend. My daddy's friend. I told Mr. Flanagan everything I knew. When I finished, my throat was dry as sawdust. The old man sat there for the longest time. He shook his head and cursed a bit.

"I always wondered," he muttered under his breath.

The old man patted me on the knee. I leaned into him, seeking comfort. He smelled of wood smoke and tobacco and safety. It was a relief to tell somebody, and I'm glad my pa sent me there.

"Now, son," he said. "I want you to go straight home. Lock the doors. Keep an eye on your mother and sister. Don't go outside, no matter what happens. As far as you're concerned, you didn't see or hear a damned thing. And you were never down in that mine. Understand? *Never!* Your life could depend on it."

I nodded. "I promise."

"Now remember what I said, Rob! This is our secret! You must never tell a soul, ever." Mr. Flanagan grabbed his cane and rose from the stoop. I watched as he hobbled towards town, then bolted home.

Things happened fast after that. The next morning, Mama and I peered out our kitchen window and saw a gathering of people on Poplar Street. I swear, every miner in town had congregated with lanterns and shovels, solemn looks on their faces. Right in the middle of the throng stood Mr. Flanagan, gesturing and shoutin' at em.

The men flowed towards The Silver Wolf, a river of miners such as I've never seen before.

Mama heard the news first. The men swarmed the shafts and tunnels like dogs on a hunt. No stone went unturned. By nightfall, they found Bill Payton's body buried beneath three feet of dirt and rocks at a steep turn in the tunnel, smoothed over to look like the ground hadn't been disturbed. The miners apprehended James O'Malley and Sheriff Johnson and brought them to justice.

Nobody could say for sure if my father had been murdered, too, but the mining company gave my mother enough money to move us back to West Virginia. Mama said we'd leave as soon as we could. I spent the remaining days with my buddy, Will, practicing our craft.

We both matured that summer. Will could hit the tin can over and over again with his spit. And I learned how to keep a secret like a man, not even telling Will or Mama what happened down in that mine shaft.

The day before we were to take the train back home, there was a knock on the door. The boy who found my red coat stood there, shuffling his feet. I opened the door a crack, then stepped out on the porch.

"This here belongs to you," the kid mumbled, holding out the jacket. "I figure you might need it."

Surprised, I took it before he could change his mind. His eyes were still surly looking, but there was something else behind 'em that looked different. He jammed his fists in his pockets and stepped off the porch.

I hollered at him. "Hey, how did you know where to find me?"

The boy stopped and turned around. His face paled beneath the sea of freckles, and he swallowed a few times before opening his mouth.

"Don't you tell nobody what I say next." He looked at the ground and poked at a tuft of grass with a boot. "Yesterday, I was sitting over yonder by the cemetery when a voice came outta nowhere. I—I looked around, but I was all alone. Plain as day, this voice whispered, *'Take the coat back to my boy, Robbie Steen, over on 7th Street.'*"

We stared at each other for a long time, the air thick with wonder. Then a train whistle split the silence and broke the spell. The boy backed away and loped across the yard, disappearing behind a house.

I clutched the coat to my heart and smiled. My father's ghost must have heard me in that mine and flew out of The Silver Wolf to save his family.

Overhead, a cloud swept by, a hard wind driving it out of Leadville. I swear to this day that it looked just like it was headin' to West Virginia, so Papa would be there waiting for us when we came home.

—Award winning author Sharon Frame Gay has been published in many anthologies and magazines, including Chicken Soup for The Soul, Typehouse, Fiction on the Web, Literally Stories, Lowestoft Chronicle, Thrice Fiction, Saddlebag Dispatches, Crannog, Owl Hollow Press *and others. She is a Pushcart Prize nominee and has won awards and nominations at The Writing District, Rope and Wire, Wow—Women on Writing, Texas Disabilities, Best of the Net, and The Peacemaker Award. Sharon was awarded The Will Rogers Medallion Award for short fiction in 2021.*

JULESBURG BURNING

CANDACE SIMAR

MY MAMA SOMETIMES had dreams that came true. She dreamed that Papa was conscripted into the Union Army. We moved to prairie country just before all men under forty were drafted, married or not. She dreamed this place along the South Platte River near Julesburg, Colorado Territory. Papa teased and called her a witch, but his eyes sparkled with love for Mama, dreams, and all.

It was winter 1865, and the Johnny rebs were taking a licking. I belonged in school, but instead, I shivered in the corn field with Papa and the boys. The livery stable was buying, and we needed the money. Papa kept us out of school to gather the standing corn in the field.

"Finish up, Viney." Papa tightened the harness and made ready to haul another load of cobs to town, only a mile away. "I'll be back for the last load around noon. You're in charge of your brothers. Keep them working."

It wasn't easy being the oldest. Asher and Oak were squirrelly on the best of days, and impossible with Papa gone. The prairie wind tangled my skirts. I wore so many shawls and sweaters that I felt round as a pumpkin. My hands blistered from stripping the sharp stalks.

Papa slapped the lines and waved.

"Bring us some candy?" I needed something to bribe the boys into action. "Please."

Papa's wink promised a bag of peppermints at the end of the day. "Boys, mind your sister. Don't pester your mother. She's taking a lie-down with the baby."

Forrest was only three weeks old, and colicky. He kept Mama awake half the night. The birth had not gone well, and I worried about her. Women died in childbed all the time.

If something happened to Mama, I'd be stuck caring for the younger ones. Mama knew how to time important tasks. She baked, cleaned, washed clothes, gardened, and made soap. She knew when to clean the chimney and how to weave cloth. Her hands were never quiet. When she wasn't working at some chore, she was knitting or praying the rosary. Or knitting and praying. I could never manage without her, though Magda Sundstrom was doing just that since her mother had died in childbed.

We each picked another long row, dragging gunny sacks for the cobs. My fingers ached and Asher's cheeks bloomed red from the wind. Oak wiped his runny nose on his sleeve. He was only nine years old, and too short to reach the top ears. I finished my row and helped him finish his.

"Viney, Viney Jane Randall." Mama stood in the doorway of the soddy, shielding the baby with a blanket. Her rosary beads twined around her arm. She looked pale as milk and gripped the side of the frame for support. "Come, I need you."

Mama wobbled, and I rushed to rescue the baby. He smelled of spit-up, but cuddled sweet and warm in my arms. "Are you sick?"

"I had a dream."

A chill went down my spine. "What kind of dream?" I hugged the baby closer to my chest.

"I'm still shaking, it was so...." Mama slumped into a chair.

I fetched a blanket to throw around her shoulders and poured a cup of coffee from the pot on the stove. I settled the baby in his cradle before sitting down across from her.

"It was just a bad dream," I said. Asher and Oak dallied in the field. I saw them through the window. Papa would be mad if the work wasn't finished. "Don't worry. Everything is fine."

"Don't tell me it's fine when it's not." Mama set her jaw and clenched her fist. Forrest fussed in the cradle. "The fire needs tending."

I poked sticks in the stove box, thankful for the cottonwoods that grew along the river and provided us with wood.

"I saw Indian warriors weeping over their dead families. They mourned for a long time, and then made war on the whites." Her voice trailed off and she looked toward the trail Papa had taken. "In my dream, they burned Julesburg to the ground. Every last house of it."

Papa was in Julesburg. I swallowed hard. Mama was too weak from childbed to think straight. She was out of her head.

"It was only a dream."

"I know the voice of God." Mama kissed the rosary and put it into her apron pocket. She prayed the rosary every day, and sometimes twice. On the day Forrest was born, she prayed all day long without stopping: *Pray for us sinners, now, and in the hour of our death.* She made anyone nearby pray it with her. The decades stretched as long as the waiting rows of corn.

"Papa said to pick the corn."

"The corn will wait." She straightened her spine like a general issuing orders. "We don't have much time."

The boys cheered to leave the cornfield. I wasn't so sure. Papa expected another load waiting when he returned. Mama swayed on her feet, but she barked orders with great determination.

Mama sent Asher to draw two buckets of water from the well and put them in the root cellar. The root cellar tucked into a small hill behind the barn. We used it to store cabbages and potatoes. We sheltered in it during summer storms. It smelled like a grave, and spiders and snakes lurked in its corners.

Mama's lips set into a hard slash. Nothing would stop her when she took a notion. "We have to move out of the soddy. Empty the cupboards, Viney. Put everything in the washtub."

"Everything?" I stood gaping. Mama was delirious. Maybe she had childbed fever. A dream was only a dream—most of the time.

"The Indians will take anything left inside. Don't you understand? Remember the Scripture passage from Isaiah 30:21, *You will hear a voice in your ear, this is the way, walk ye in it.* It's in my ear and I'm duty-bound to obey."

Ridiculous. Crazy. I dawdled, hoping Papa would come home and put a stop to Mama's plan. I stacked canned goods, spices, sugar, salt, tea, coffee, grinder, and cornmeal in the washtub.

Mama looked terrible, thin, and pale as a ghost. I imagined Mama on her death bed, reaching out a bony hand and asking me to take care of the family. I pictured Forrest crying because he was hungry. He became weaker and died in his cradle without Mama's milk. We would have to find a wet nurse among the neighbors to save his life.

"No dallying, Viney. I mean it."

The baby shrieked, pulling up his legs with colic. Mama didn't pay attention to him at first. Then, she asked Oak to hold the small child while she collected clothes, blankets, dishes, knives, spoons, and pots. She packed them in the wheelbarrow, which was full to the brim.

Mama added the family Bible, the candles, and the tubs of soap made after the butchering. Then she unfastened the crucifix from its place above the door.

Mama pushed the wheelbarrow while I lugged the washtub. How silly to leave our warm house for a hole in the ground. Mama lit a candle and placed it on a holder stuck into the earthen wall. Asher lugged the water buckets, his face sweaty from hurrying. Mama covered them with a cloth and put them to one side where they would be out of the way.

"Milk the cow and gather the eggs," she said to Asher. "Put Flossie out to pasture. Open the chicken pen and chase the fowl into the cottonwoods by the river. Don't lollygag."

"It's too early for the milking." Asher's forehead furrowed. "Pa says the coyotes will get the hens if they're free to roam.

"Mind me," Mama said.

Asher shrugged. "Don't blame me if Papa gets mad."

Mama shielded her eyes with one hand and scanned the prairie around us. She spent a long moment looking across the river. The wind rustled the brown grass and rippled the water. Everyone and everything was ordinary, except for Mama. She stood there, wild-haired and determined, like a prophet from the Bible.

It was almost noon, but Mama said nothing about dinner. We had been in the field since daybreak, and my stomach growled. I looked toward Julesburg, hoping Papa would come down the trail. My breath caught, worrying about him alone with trouble on its way. I shook my head of the dark thoughts. Mama's dream meant nothing.

Back at the soddy, Oak jiggled the crying baby. "He wants you, Mama. He wet all over my trousers." Oak looked ready to cry. "Can't you take him?"

"He'll have to wait," Mama said. "Let him suck your finger."

Oak stuck a knuckle into Forrest's mouth and the fussing stopped. Mama was so pre-occupied with her dream that she hadn't noticed Oak's filthy hands.

Mama eyed the large crock of brined pork and the flour barrel. "These are too heavy to lift into the wheelbarrow. We'll drag them onto the stone boat."

Papa would be mad if Mama lifted anything heavy so close after Forrest's birth. I pressed my thin shoulder to the task. We pulled the heavy crock onto the flat wooden sledge that Papa used to gather rocks. The smelly brine spilled on me, making my dress wet and my legs cold. The wind whirled our aprons and petticoats. Mama's hair blew out of its pins. It framed her face like a wild woman. Like a witch. I shivered from more than winter winds.

We pulled the sledge until I thought my eyeballs would pop out of my head, but made little progress. The load was too heavy. Mama looked ready to collapse.

"Would be easier if it had wheels," I said when we stopped for a breather. "We could wait for Papa to bring the team."

Mama looked up at the noonday sun. "It's time for the Angelus." She dropped to her knees and motioned me to join her in noon prayers. *"The Angel of the Lord declared unto Mary."*

"And she conceived of the Holy Spirit," I said as I knelt on the frozen ground. The words of the prayer rolled over me. What would Papa say? Would Mama's dream happen? God could stop all the trouble if He wanted. Why did they have to pray for Him to act?

Mama finished her prayers and rose to her feet, her face relaxed.

"They'll find us." The fresh grooves from the wheelbarrow and the sledge marked a plain trail to the root cellar. My voice squeaked as I pointed to the tracks. "Even if we hide in the root cellar."

"Trust God," Mama said. "Surrender your will to His."

Forrest wailed. Asher brought a sloshing milk bucket. Mama fetched Oak and the baby. She placed the baby on a quilt out of the way, and covered him with another.

"Pray, children. Ask for God's strength," Mama said.

The boys pushed, and Mama and I pulled, the heavy sledge inch by inch up the small rise that led to the cellar. *Glory be to the Father, and to the Son, and to the Holy Ghost.* Somehow, we did it. It didn't mean Mama's dream was real. It didn't mean God had answered our prayers.

We made a second trip with the flour barrel. "Our food is safe at least." Mama paused to catch her breath, hanging on to the rim of the barrel for support. Tears glistened on her face in the candlelight. "I've always feared not having food for you children. How good of the Lord God to warn in time."

The baby screamed and Mama nursed him from a seat on the woodpile outside the root cellar. Little Forrest gulped milk and clutched Mama's dress with his chubby hand.

"Fetch the corn sacks," Mama said. "I'll help after the baby's asleep."

We met Papa on our way to the cornfield. His empty wagon rattled behind the horses. Papa eyed the sacks already picked. His mouth set into a grimace and he looked at us with displeasure written across his face.

"Not even half a load," he said. "Have you been fiddling around?"

"It's Mama's fault." I thought of the candy in his pocket, the reward for our labor. "She's all worked up about a dream, and has kept us running ever since you left."

"She made me chase the hens into the cottonwoods." Asher's lip quivered. "I told her the coyotes would get them."

"And she made us put Flossie out to pasture." Oak always lisped his s's. "And the baby wet all over my pants."

"She's out of her head," I whispered. "Acting strange."

"I'll sort it out," Papa said. "Where is she?"

We pointed to the root cellar and followed Papa with the corn sacks balanced on our backs. His eyes widened when we passed the empty soddy with its door sagging open on its leather hinges.

"Did you gather the eggs like I told you?" Mama still sat on the woodpile with the baby at her breast. Asher hung his head. She didn't even say hello to Papa. "Run along, then. Oak, help your brother."

"What's going on, Em?" Papa's voice was the tone used to soothe a crying child or a wild heifer.

Mama shoved the baby into my arms and told me to change his diaper. I took him into the root cellar and laid him on top of a sack of potatoes. Poor baby was soaked. Though I didn't mean to eavesdrop, I heard their entire conversation.

"What's the news in town?" Mama said. "I know it's bad."

Papa hesitated and cleared his throat. "I ran into the Perkins boy who took a new job at Fort Rankin."

"And?"

"Seems the Cheyenne are stirred up from that skirmish at Sand Creek." Papa's voice sounded old and weary. "They've been raiding all around us, and that Perkins kid—is his name Joshua? He said they're teamed up with the Arapaho and Lakota. He claims a thousand warriors are hell-bent for revenge. Joshua sneaked away to warn his folks."

A thousand Indians. We wouldn't have a chance against them. They could come any time and murder us in our beds. Sometimes they kidnapped babies and little kids to raise as their own. Sometimes they stole girls my age for wives. They would need both wives and children to replace the ones killed by the soldiers. I pulled Forrest closer. He smelled sweeter with his diaper changed. Lucky boy was too young to understand, too small to worry.

"The murder of women and children is more than a skirmish,"

Mama said. "I saw it in my dream." Her voice broke. I tipped my head to see Papa wrap his arms around her. "They were weeping over their dead families, grown men wailing and shaking their fists."

I pictured Indian warriors kneeling beside their fallen wives and children. I swallowed a lump in my throat and kissed the top of Forrest's head.

"Damn Chivington should be brought up on charges. Murdering women and children. Makes you wonder how civilized we are," Papa said. "He should go back and fight the Johnny Rebs. He's done enough damage in this country."

"I saw Julesburg burning to the ground." Mama whispered. "A warning from God."

Asher and Oak came running with the egg basket. Mama lowered her voice until I no longer heard their conversation. Papa stepped inside the root cellar, bending low to avoid hitting his head on the door frame. The candle burned low.

"Mama made us move everything out of the soddy," I said. "I told her we were supposed to pick the corn."

"It's crowded in here." He pushed the flour barrel into the corner and pulled the salt pork crock in front of it to make more room.

"She's acting crazy."

"I won't have you speaking ill of your mother."

"It won't help to hide in the root cellar," I said. "We left a trail that a blind man could follow. And we can't live without a fire."

Papa kissed the top of Forrest's head, and then mine.

"What if it's a dream?" I had to make Papa understand. "What if all this is for nothing?"

"It won't hurt us to camp out in the cellar a few days. Your mother says she heard from the Lord." He took a deep breath and looked at me with pleading eyes. "She wouldn't say it unless she thought it to be true."

He left the root cellar and I heard him telling Mama to take a rest.

I wrapped Forrest in a dry blanket and tucked him in his cradle. Outside, Mama sat on the woodpile. She shivered in the cold, and I fetched a blanket and draped it over her shoulders.

"Papa told you to have a lie-down," I said.

"I'm too worked up to sleep."

Papa watered the team at the river, still in harness. Afterwards he hitched them to a giant cottonwood tree that had gone down in last summer's storm.

"What's he doing?" Mama craned her neck as the horses pulled the dead tree toward them. "He'll be wanting dinner, and the boys must be starving. Bread and leftover potatoes will do. It's a good thing I did the baking yesterday."

"Potato and onion sandwiches. Papa likes them with mustard." I balanced the cutting board on top of the flour barrel for a makeshift table. The knives were in the bread box where Mama had put them. I couldn't find the mustard pot. Soon onions masked the earthen smell that reminded me, too much, of a grave.

I brought the sandwiches outside. The boys came running. Mama nibbled on a crust. Papa wolfed down one sandwich, and then another. The cottonwood splayed a spidery mess of roots. The treetop held dead leaves in its massive branches.

"I'll pull the tree in front of the cellar door. We'll stack wood on the wheelbarrow and stone boat nearby. The Indians will attribute the tracks to hauling firewood. We'll crawl into the cellar from the backside of the tree. Indians won't see the door unless they crawl under the branches and look for it."

Papa was smart. I rested easier, then, with Papa taking charge.

"Do you have ammunition for your long gun?" Mama said.

"Enough," Papa said. "And I have my sidearm."

I shivered to think of Papa shooting at Indians who were shooting back. We could all die. I wouldn't graduate from eighth grade or have a beau or get kissed. The baby would never know how much we loved him. The little boys would never grow up. A fierce anger settled into my gut. I wanted a sidearm, too, to protect Mama and the boys. I wouldn't let something happen to them.

"I WAS SORRY to see this beautiful tree go down last summer." Mama's voice slipped into a dreamy sing-song. She looked off into the distance with sad eyes. "I never imagined God planned for it to save us."

We practiced crawling underneath the treetop to reach the door. Papa piled firewood around gaps in the branches.

"There," Mama folded her arms and smiled at Papa with lips as blue as her eyes. "We're ready."

"Now, Em," Papa said in a measured tone. "We can't live without a fire. The baby might catch lung fever without heat. And we need hot food."

"We'll be fine," Mama said. "It won't be long."

"We could go into Julesburg once the army whips the Indians."

I could go back to school if we moved into town. I waited for Papa to convince her.

"Didn't you hear me?" Mama spat out the words and anger sparked her eyes. "I told you that Julesburg is going up in flames."

"They're forewarned," Papa said. "Forty townspeople have taken up arms. Julesburg won't be overrun."

"It will burn." Mama pulled the rosary out of her pocket. "I saw it."

"Fort Rankin would be safer until the trouble is over," Papa said. "We'll stay here a night or two, and then pack up for the fort."

Mama fingered the beads as she mouthed the prayers.

"Lie down, Em," Papa said. "I insist. You're exhausted."

Mama obeyed, still fingering the beads. I stayed with Mama and the baby in the root cellar, trying to rearrange things to make more room. Papa and the boys tethered the team out of sight of the house, in a thicket of brush.

Towards supper time, Papa made a small fire in the soddy for everyone to warm themselves. How good it felt. Warming stones heated for our beds. Papa cooked coffee and a pot of oatmeal. I fried bacon while Papa drank the coffee. Though it was still light, we trudged to the root cellar like a bunch of gypsies. I carried the hot frying pan. Papa clutched the rifle in one hand and the mush pot in the other. The boys carried the hot stones wrapped in flannel.

It was as dark as night inside the cellar until Papa lit another candle. We crowded on top of each other. Oak and Asher argued until Papa placed the cradle on the flour barrel. He did this to make space for the sacks of potatoes that the boys slept on. Mama and Papa had their mattress from the soddy. There was no place for me. Mama moved closer to Papa and lay Forrest on her chest. Then she patted the mattress beside her, like when I was little. I snuggled up to her, trying to forget about dreams and nightmares, and how to tell them apart.

There were so many things I didn't understand. Soldiers, baptized Christians, who massacred women and children. A thousand heathen Indians seeking revenge. Fort Rankin couldn't stand against such a number. I didn't understand about God or prayers or why some women died giving birth. Mama prayed the rosary, and I drifted to sleep with the sound of her voice in my ear.

Later, Papa got up and crept to the door. He cracked it open and listened. Cold air rushed in and the boys stirred on their potato sacks.

Mama held Forrest to her breast. He made loud sucking sounds while nursing, putting our hiding spot at risk.

"What's the matter, Hugo?" Mama whispered anxiously. "Do you hear something?"

"I thought I heard hoofbeats."

"What time is it?" I asked.

"Almost sunrise," Papa said. "Pink edge in the east."

"It's freezing," Mama said. "Come back to bed."

Papa lingered at the door a bit longer. "It *is* hoofbeats," he said. "Sounds like an army coming." He latched the door and sat in front of it, rifle in hand. His outline showed in the glimmer of the candle stub. "Viney, put out the candle. We don't want light showing through the cracks in the door."

Guttural voices sounded from outside along with the sounds of horses. A person yelled near the soddy, a loud whoop. We heard horses galloping towards the river. The ground beneath us trembled.

They were looking for us. I held my breath. Forrest pulled away from Mama's breast and let out a cry. Mama poked her breast into his open mouth and quieted him. The boys slept through the commotion. I wished I were asleep. I wished I were too young to understand the danger.

Victory cries and whoops sounded outside. "Do they see the door?" I imagined them bursting through while brandishing knives and hatchets. I snugged closer to Mama and felt the steady beat of her heart. She fingered her rosary beads and mouthed the words.

"They found the team," Papa whispered. "Damn them."

More howling and war cries. We hid underground like mice, hardly daring to breathe. We were inches away from certain death. *Pray for us sinners, now, and in the hour of our death.* Was this our hour? I prayed with her, the ancient words a comfort.

We heard them leaving. Our poor horses, such good and faithful beasts. How would the Cheyenne treat them? I thought of my school and the friends who lived in town. Would they survive this day?

We heard the crack of gunfire and war whoops in the distance. Blasts of a cannon boomed like a summer storm. Papa peeked out the door. "They burned the wagons. Couldn't do much damage to the sod barn or house, but the devils had to find some mischief."

We stayed underground the whole day, but Papa ventured out later that afternoon with his rifle in hand. Her returned with the bad news that it was Flossie who the Cheyenne had killed. The team was still tethered out of sight. "We can still use her meat, but it means no milk for the children."

I felt like crying. Flossie was part of the family. I couldn't remember a time when she didn't provide milk and butter for our table. There were times when it was all we had. But they spared the horses. Thank God for that. Papa got ready to salvage the beef. He found the empty dishpan, the butcher knives, and Mama's mixing bowl. "I can at least take the liver and tongue. More if the Indians don't come back." I offered to go with him.

"Stay here and take care of your mother and the boys," he said. "Smoke rises over Julesburg."

"Mama, your dream." God had spoken to Mama. "It was the voice of the Lord speaking to you."

She squeezed my hand and smiled. She held up her rosary with her other hand. *"And the Lord spoke to Samuel in a dream."*

"Your mama's dreams," Papa said.

Even in the dim light I saw his shining eyes. He bent down and kissed Mama's face. "Can you believe I had the good sense to marry a dreamer?"

—Candace Simar likes to imagine how things might have been. Her historical fiction and short stories combine her love of story and passion for history. Simar's work has been recognized with a WWA Spur Award, Will Rogers Gold Medallion, Western Fictioneers Peacemaker Award, Laura Awards in Short Fiction, Finalist Willa Literary Award in Historical Fiction, Finalist Midwest Book Award, and other regional awards. Sister Lumberjack, *Book 5 of the Abercrombie Trail Series, was released March 2024. Watch for her column "Best Writing Tips" in* Roundup Magazine. *Candace lives in Minnesota. www.candacesimar.com*

The Enemies' Horses by W. Herbert Dunton

THE BONES OF A FOOL

TERRY CAMPBELL

"YOU DON'T SEEM too happy for a man who's just inherited six-hundred acres of pure untamed frontier wilderness," William Gadsen said to his client. "This part of Colorado is booming, what with the gold rush and all."

"Is it now?" Clinton Daniels responded. He propped his boot up on a large boulder, hands on his hips, and surveyed the rocky landscape. The Sawatch Mountains loomed in the distance, the great peaks of Mount Elbert and Mount Massive shrouded in a purple, shimmering haze on the horizon. Deep ravines cut into the stoney surface in jagged crooks. "You wouldn't know it by looking around this land."

"Well, six-hundred acres is a lot of land to inspect. You've barely scratched the surface. Sounds like you're giving up a little prematurely to me."

Clinton gave the man a wary look. "I stopped in for a drink earlier at the Slag House Saloon. They 'bout laughed me out of town when I told them whose land I'd inherited."

Gadsen sighed. "You're Uncle Tyson *was* viewed as sort of an eccentric around these parts, that's for sure. But don't let that cloud your judgement over what you have here."

Clinton turned and spread his arms wide and slowly turned in circles. He laughed out loud. "What have we here? What we have is a giant graveyard for critters of some sort. A big pile of bones sticking out of rocks as far as the eye can see. And looking at the size of all these giant crevices, I'd say a pretty big muddy mess any time it rains."

"It wasn't 'til a few years ago when that big quake hit up in Fort Collins that the land opened up like this. It was good land for a nice horse ranch before that. But your uncle, for all his quirkiness, could be quite a shrewd businessman. Perhaps you should learn from his approach."

Clinton smirked. "Oh, yeah? Like what?"

"Well, sometimes all you can do is play the hand you're dealt." Gadsen answered.

"What the hell's *that* supposed to mean?"

"It means, take what you have. Figure out something to do with it. After this land got busted up like this, your uncle switched directions. Tyson often brought folks out here to look at all these bones. He was toying with the idea of starting up a park, giving tours and charging people a dime a head."

Clinton spat a stream of tobacco on an exposed bone. "My uncle was a damned fool."

"Well, perhaps that sealed envelope I gave you earlier might shed some light on the situation. Tyson said you were to read that first thing. Might explain a lot."

Clinton looked at the envelope in his sweaty hand. He had forgotten he was holding it. The paper was now damp from his perspiration. A blob of red wax sealed the flap. Clinton crumpled it and shoved the envelope into his vest pocket. "I'm sure it's just some more of his insane ramblings."

"Well, whether or not you decide to stay here or sell your land, there's one good thing to keep in mind."

"Oh," Clinton said. "What's that?"

"There's growing unrest between the Ute tribe and the settlers of the area. They feel the white man continues to encroach upon their lands due to the greed of the gold."

"So, what's that got to do with me?"

Gadsen knelt and picked up what appeared to be a rocky tooth. "The Utes won't come near this land. They think all these bones are the bones of devils, that that quake opened up a portal to Hell."

"Interesting," Clinton said.

"It's a good selling point, anyway. I'll be leaving for Denver in the morning. Until my return, my advice to you, Mister Daniels, is to stay in town a few days and give your next move some serious thought. You may be sitting on more than you realize."

ERNIE "BUSTER" MAGEE gently placed the gold nugget on the counter at Downing's Dry Goods in downtown Leadville and stepped back, beaming from head to toe. Mr. Downing looked first at the nugget, then back to Buster and grinned.

"Buster Magee, I declare, did you find another nugget out there on your daddy's property? Excuse me, your property?"

Buster's smile grew even wider, if that was possible, and he nodded his head vigorously. "I surely did, Mister Downing!"

The proprietor picked up the nugget and held it up to the sunlight glaring in through the front windows and whistled in awe. "Lord almighty, would you look at that? Fellers, just look at this beaut," he said to his other customers.

The folks in the store gathered around Buster and patted him on the back. A few ruffled his shaggy hair. Mrs. Wilkins gave him a quick peck on the cheek, causing Buster's face to grow bright shades of crimson.

Everyone in town looked upon Buster Magee as their own kin. His father had passed away a few months earlier, leaving his 150 acres southwest of town to his only offspring. Buster was a bit slow on the draw mentally, and everyone took it upon themselves to look after their favorite son. And of course, everyone knew that the "gold" that Buster was finding on his daddy's land was just pyrite—fool's gold, but the town took care of any needs he had, and letting Buster think he was finding real gold out there gave the slow-witted young man his own sense of worth. It was the least they could do. Dalton Magee had been much loved by the citizens of Leadville, and they had always done what they could to help look after his challenged son.

"Well, Buster," Mr. Downing said. "This little rock will more than pay for these little bits of goods you brung to the counter." The store owner winked at the nearest customer. "And then some."

"Well, all right, Mister Downing. That will be just fine."

"You figure out yet what you're gonna do with all that land?"

Buster nodded his head enthusiastically. "I'm going to build a little house for me and Penelope. And then maybe we'll raise goats."

"Buster Magee, goat farmer," Mr. Downing laughed. "That sounds like a right good plan, son. I'm sure you and your little bride will be very happy. And then, maybe you'll work on a family of your own, huh?" Mr. Downing reached out and poked Buster's shoulder.

The young man blushed hard and dropped his gaze to the floor. "Awww, shucks, Mister Downing. I don't know about that."

The shoppers all laughed at that, and Buster grabbed his purchases and, still grinning ear to ear, scurried past the customers—a stranger among them he did not recognize—and out the door and onto the streets of Leadville.

"HEY, STRANGER, I got a bone to pick with you."

The rowdy crowd inside the Slag House erupted into hysterics. Clinton smiled and tipped his hat to the crowd, motioned to the bartender for a whiskey, and took a seat at a table near the front window in order to see out into the streets of Leadville. Someone had been kind enough to leave a recent edition of *The Reveille* on the table, so Clinton occupied himself by thumbing through the paper for any interesting tidbits. After a moment, one of the saloon girls sat his glass of whiskey on the table.

Clinton looked up and gave her a wink. "What do I owe you?"

"Already taken care of, sweetie," she said, returning the gesture and thumbing toward a table at the back of the saloon. A dapperly dressed gentleman lifted his own libation toward Clinton and stood.

"Mister Clinton Daniels, am I correct? May I join you?"

Clinton motioned to the empty chair across from him. "You've earned that privilege, I'd say. Thank you for the drink, Mister...?"

"Standish. Archibald Standish," he said, offering his hand to Clinton. "I wish to apologize for the sledgehammer wit of this establishment's patrons. I'm afraid they are quick to pounce on what they perceive to be the less fortunate in order to escape their own mundane existences, if only temporarily."

Clinton took a sip from his tumbler. "Oh, they're just having a bit of fun with the new kid in town. No harm done, I suppose."

Standish retrieved two cigars from his vest pocket and proffered one to Clinton. "Pardon my saying so, Mister Standish," Clinton said, taking the smoke, "but you seem a bit more distinguished and eloquent than the heap of this saloon's clientele. May I ask what you do here in Leadville?"

"I'm an attorney," Standish answered. "I specialize in land holdings and domestic affairs."

Clinton struck a match on the table and lit his cigar. He leaned back in the chair and trained his eyes on his new friend. "Land holdings, huh? Is that what this is about?"

Standish smiled. "I understand you've come in to quite a bit of property. Tyson Daniels' land, to be specific. You aim to keep that land, move out here to Colorado?"

Clinton smirked. "I come from Kentucky, Mister Standish, where God chose to put trees on the mountains. Not the scrubby sticks out on that pile of rocks."

"I'll take that as a 'no', then." The attorney took a sip of his whiskey and paused, then continued. "So, what are your plans, if you don't mind my asking?"

"I'm not real sure," Clinton answered. "My attorney is in Denver for a few days. He asked me to stay and mull my decision over."

"Who is your attorney?"

"William Gadsen." Clinton could read something in Standish's eyes at that moment. "What? What about Gadsen?"

Standish shook his head. "Not my style to talk about one of my peers," he said. "But since you asked, he has little sense of land values. No instinct."

"And you do?"

"How would you like to swap your acreage for something that may prove a bit more... lucrative?"

"Maybe I'm listening."

Standish took his cigar between his fingers and looked about the saloon, as if checking who might be within earshot. He leaned forward and motioned for Clinton to do the same. "I represent the Magee estate. Have for many years. Old man Dalton passed a few years ago and left his entire estate to his son, Ernie. All of my faithful years of trusted service, and he left me nothing. Gave it all to that imbecilic offspring of his."

"Wait a minute," Clinton said. "I saw someone in the general store earlier buying supplies with what looked like a gold nugget. He's kind of slow on the uptake, right?"

"That was Ernie. Buster, everyone in town calls him. Old Dalton only had a hundred and fifty acres, but they've busted more gold out of those rocks than I care to hear about."

Clinton squinted his eyes and studied those of his drinking partner. "What exactly do you have up your sleeve, Mister Standish?"

"Please, call me Archibald. Hell, call me Archie. We're about to be business partners." The two men made a quick toast. "No, Ernie trusts me implicitly and, like I've already stated, he's a fool. He'll take my word for anything. I can convince him to swap land holdings with you, straight up. No cash involved. I can draw up the papers, we can sign them, and it'll be done before anyone is any the wiser."

"Now, hold up just a minute," Clinton said. "He gets six hundred acres, and I get a hundred and fifty?"

Standish perused the bar again and returned his gaze to Clinton. "You get a hundred and fifty *gold-rich* acres. He gets six hundred piles of rocks and bones."

"Well, how do I know for sure that there's not any gold on *my* six hundred acres?"

"Mister Daniels, I ask you, was your uncle Tyson a rich man?"

Clinton shrugged. "No."

"He'd been on that land for twenty something years. Don't you think he'd have found something, anything, in all that time? And, in the meantime, that idiot Ernie is bringing in a nugget every couple of weeks. Boy don't have to pay for nothing around here."

"I suppose so."

"Now, let's discuss my fee. If I make this happen, then I get a cut of whatever you bring out of there. Old man Dalton didn't cut me in on a thing. I want twenty percent, sound fair?"

Clinton stared out on the streets of Leadville for a long moment.

"You'll not get this kind of opportunity again, Mister Daniels. We have to do this quick, before Gadsen gets back into town. He'll shut it down for sure. And not a word to anyone in town. This town protects that dim-wit like an old mother hen. Especially Marshall Duggan. He'd throw us in the jail or shoot us dead, whichever he thinks of first. So, this conversation never happened. You leave the rest to me. And whatever you do, just lay low. This can be a rough town."

BUSTER STOOD ATOP one of the higher crags of rock and peered out over the horizon, using his worn old hat to block the sun. He could see mountains in the distance, and lots of valleys and ridges between here and there.

"So, what do you think, Ernie?" Achibald Standish asked.

"I don't know, Mister Standish. It looks really rocky."

"Well, no more than where you're at now, I'd say. And you'd quadruple your land ownings."

Buster turned and looked back down on the other two men. "What's Quadruple?"

"It means four times, Buster," Clinton said to the slow man. "You would have four times as much land as you have now."

Buster whistled. "Golly, is there gold here?"

Clinton and Standish exchanged glances. "Well, I'm sure there is. You remember Tyson, right? He was always out here digging."

Buster scooted down the craggy rocks and stopped before the two men, pausing to brush the dust from his trousers. "You haven't started building your house yet, right?"

"No," Buster said. "I've ordered some timber from the general store, but Mister Downing said it might take a few months for it to get here."

"Well, that's perfect then," Standish said. "That's plenty of time to get all the proper paperwork together."

Buster kicked at one of the bones protruding from the rock. "What's with all these weird rocks? What are they?"

"Devil bones," Clinton said. "Bones from long dead dragons."

Buster gasped. "Then this land is bad. No thank you."

"No, no, no, no," Clinton said. "It's a *good* thing, Ernie. They've been dead for hundreds of years. They can't hurt you."

"Ernie, I hear you had some troubles with some Injuns out on your property last week," Standish added. "Any truth to that?"

Buster shrugged. "I reckon so. Someone stole some things I had sitting out on my property. Busted up that old building my daddy built."

"That's a damn shame."

"Well, you don't want to build a house for you and your young bride out there, Ernie," the attorney continued. "That's too close to the Utes' territory. Even your daddy always feared that. That's why you need this land. This is where you want to bring your timber and build your house."

Standish knelt and picked up a piece of the petrified bone. It was about four inches long, and what appeared to be several sharp teeth protruded from the matrix. A jawbone.

"And this is why," he said, handing the bone to Buster.

"The Utes are afraid of this land. They won't come near it. They think these ancient devils and dragons are what chased their kin from the mountains out yonder.

"You and Penelope will be safe out here, Ernie. Your new family will thrive here with no worries. It's what your daddy would've wanted for you. Trust me. Have I ever steered your family wrong?"

Buster dropped the jawbone to the ground, chipping the point of one of the teeth. "No, sir."

Archibald Standish placed his hand on Buster's skinny shoulder. "You're doing the right thing, son. We'll get the papers drawn up and this will be all yours by morning."

"I MUST SAY I'm a bit disappointed, Mister Daniels," Gadsen said. "I asked you to not make any decisions until I'd returned from Denver."

He looked down at the two men sitting at the same table where their initial meeting had transpired, smoking the celebratory cigar and enjoying a rare glass of sotol. "As for you, Mister Standish, I would say it is not disappointing, but expected."

Standish lifted his glass to his peer. "In this market, in this day and age, one must strike quickly. Any lawyer worth his weight in gold should know that." He looked at Clinton, and the two men burst into laughter. "And I'd say that weight may soon increase exponentially."

Gadsen lifted his eyebrows. "Oh, is *that* was this is about?"

Standish lifted the glass to his lips and drained the contents, releasing a satisfying "aaaaah." He motioned for the bartender to bring another round.

"You swindled that poor boy out of his land, land that had been in his family for decades? For the gold he's been finding out there?"

"I think Ernie made out pretty well for himself. Quadrupled his land holdings with the flick of the quill. Of course, a fool and his gold are soon parted, as it were." He maintained his gaze into the eyes of his peer. "Feel free to look the papers over. Finalized and perfectly legal."

"Oh, I suspect everything is in order," Gadsen said. "I would've signed them myself if given the opportunity."

Clinton looked up from his drink. "You would've signed Buster's land over to me?"

"Of course," he answered. "As your new attorney mentioned prior, Buster quadrupled his land, and as far as a fool's gold . . . Well, that's exactly what he lost."

Standish and Clinton's eyes met. Each could read the concern on the others' faces. "What do you mean, a *fool's* gold?"

"I mean exactly that. Fool's gold. Pyrite."

"Wait a minute, what do you mean?" Clinton said, standing.

"You think Buster's been finding real gold out on his property? Correction, *your* property?"

"What, you mean that ain't real gold?" Clinton asked.

Standish was stunned. "But I've seen him bring it in. He's shown it to me. Every time he finds a nugget, he shows it to me like it's a newborn baby." Standish stammered. "How has he been making all those purchases? The timber for his house?"

"This town loved Dalton Magee. And they love Buster. We take care of the less fortunate around here, Archie. We don't swindle them. As a matter of fact, you didn't swindle him at all. Buster swindled *you.*"

"We all knew what was going on, Standish," a large, looming figure said as it approached. "We just let you dig your own grave."

Marshall Mart Duggan tapped a meaty fist on the table. Clinton jumped and sat back down. "I ought to run you both in, but I think the situation has played itself out admirably, what do you think, Archie?"

"After all I've done for Leadville," Standish mumbled. "This is how I'm treated. I'm the overseer of the Magee estate. Why was I not told the truth about this so-called fool's gold?"

"Because Dalton Magee never trusted you," Gadsen answered. "He stipulated in his will that we were to watch your every move when it came to his holdings."

"You idiot," Clinton said to Standish. "Now, my land has shrunk to practically nothing."

"And Mister Daniels," the Marshall said. "I'm trying to clear my town of unscrupulous characters such as yourself, not bring more in. I suggest you rid yourself of that land and tuck your tail back to where it come from." He then turned to Standish. "As for *you,* Archie—you can either help Buster build his new house, or you can take your questionable practice to another town. Your choice."

At that moment, there was a commotion from outside. Dust swirled in clouds, obscuring the buildings across the street. The Slag House emptied in seconds, everyone vying for a clear vantage point. Hats flew from heads in the swirling winds, dust pellets flew into eyes. When the air finally cleared, a line of six flat wagons pulled by large muscular stallions had pulled into town. A man with a balding head and long dark beard stepped from the lead wagon. He stopped long enough to knock some dust from his person and then headed toward the saloon.

Spying the Marshall's badge, the man approached. "Ah, Marshall, can you direct me to a man by the name of Tyson Daniels, please?"

"Who may I ask is calling?" Duggan asked.

The man extended his hand. "My name is Othniel Charles Marsh. I have business with Mister Daniels."

"Well," the Marshall began, "I'm sorry to be the one to tell you this, but Tyson Daniels passed away a few months ago."

The new arrival removed his hat and bowed his head. The crowd grew silent, allowing the man to pay his respects. After a moment, Marsh lifted his head. "I was afraid that might come to pass. He mentioned in his letters that he had grown quite ill."

"His letters?" Gadsen asked.

"Yes, I've been in contact with Tyson for nearly a year. We were working on a possible business transaction."

Gadsen rubbed his chin. "He hadn't mentioned anything to me. Oh, I'm sorry, Mister Marsh." He extended his hand. "William Gadsen. I was Tyson's attorney."

"Pleased to meet you," Marsh said. "Sorry it's under these circumstances. But no, our dealings were hush-hush. Tyson and myself wanted it that way."

Marshall Duggan turned to the nearest observer. "Somebody go fetch Buster. I have a feeling this is about to get good."

"I've come a long way, with many a great expense," Marsh continued. "Oh, by the way, to anyone's knowledge, has a man by the name of Edward Drinker Cope visited your fair town recently?"

Muted responses and shaking heads followed. "Not that I'd heard," Marshall Duggan answered.

"Good, good. Then word has not gotten out. That's good."

"Word about what?"

"About my business with Tyson, of course. I'm sorry to ask at such a time, but what legally became of Tyson's land? Did he have an heir?"

Clinton stepped up. "That would be me," he said. "I'm his nephew, Clinton Daniels."

"Now, hold on, hoss," Duggan said. "You're his nephew, rightly. But, as you might recall, you no longer own that land, correct?"

"Oh," Marsh said. "Well, who does, if I may ask?"

"You wanted to see me, Marshall?"

The crowd parted to let a stumbling Buster Magee push through. He had gotten his boot tangled in a protruding rock. "Dangit."

Gadsen sidled up to Clinton, and with his voice low as to avoid prying ears, asked, "Clinton, did you ever read that letter your uncle left for you? The one I gave you when we first went out to look at Tyson's land?"

Clinton's eyes dropped to the toes of his boots and he shuffled in place. "No, no I didn't."

Gadsen gazed at the young man. Sheepishly, Clinton reached into his vest pocket and retrieved the envelope. He smoothed out the paper and retrieved a small buck knife from his trousers pocket. With visibly shaking hands, Clinton sliced the top of the envelope and pulled out the letter. He sighed, opened it and began to read.

Dearest nephew,

If you are reading these words, it means that I have passed on. Do not mourn me, as I am in a much better place now. You should also know by now that my six hundred acres near Leadville, Colorado belong to you. Settle there and wait. A man named Othniel Charles Marsh will be visiting you. Wait for his arrival. Whatever you do, DO NOT SELL THE LAND. This man is a scientist, and he was made aware of the copious amount of dinosaur remains on the land, and we are in negotiations for him to purchase the rights to excavate the bones before his rival beats him here. You will now negotiate the business deal. The land may have been worth very little before, but you're sitting on a potential gold mine now. Take care, dearest nephew.

Your uncle,
Tyson

Clinton had to chuckle. "Well, I'll be an asse's ass." He wadded up the letter and tossed it into the street.

"Well, Mister Magee," Marsh said to Buster. "My name is Othniel Charles Marsh. I understand you have some bones on your land. How would you like me to clear them out for you?" He took Buster's hand and shook it.

"They scare me," Buster said. "But the Indians are scared of them, too. They're devil bones."

Marshall Duggan leaned in and whispered something into Marsh's ear. The man nodded and returned his attention to Buster. "They're *not* devil bones, Buster. They're dinosaurs. It's an exciting new scientific field. These creatures lived many years ago. I collect these bones and display them in museums all across the country. I'll pay you five-hundred dollars for every specimen I collect from your land that's eighty-five percent complete or more. And I'll also pay top dollar for any interesting incomplete specimens I might find. How does that sound?"

Buster appeared confused and looked at the Marshall. "What does that mean?"

Marshall Duggan laughed and clapped the young man on the back. "It means you're about to become a rich man, Buster."

The crowd burst into laughter, and everyone approached the town's loveable simpleton and congratulated him on his fortune. Standish and Clinton attempted to slip away unnoticed.

Marshall Dugan turned and shouted. "Hey! And pick up that piece of trash before I fine you for littering."

Buster scratched his head and looked at Marsh. "So, I got dinosaurs on my new land? Not devils?"

"That's right, son," Marsh said. "And from what Tyson Daniels said in his letters, a virtual treasure trove. I can't wait to get started."

Buster turned back to the Marshall. "Will Penelope and me still be safe there, Marshall? If Mister Marsh takes the devils—I mean, the dinosaurs—away? Will the Indians still be too scared to come out there?"

"Don't worry, Buster," the Marshall said. "Nothing's changed. This town will always protect their favorite son. You can count on that."

"Hey, look who's here," someone in the crowd said.

People moved aside, and a pretty blonde-haired girl in a yellow dress ran forward and hugged Buster.

"Penelope, guess what?" Buster blurted out. "I quad—quad... *ripple...* What's that word again, Mister Standish?"

"Quadrupled?" he answered timidly.

"Yeah," Buster grinned. "Quad . . . four times, Penelope! I got four times the land my daddy had! And guess what else? We're gonna be dinosaur ranchers!"

Buster's simple enthusiasm spurred the crowd once again to laughter, and as they filed back into the Slag House to celebrate, the sun, as beautiful and stunning as any nugget of gold a fool might gaze upon, set on the town of Leadville.

—Terry Campbell is a writer/artist who lives in a tiny house in McKinney, Texas with his lovely wife and two Chinese Crested dogs. When not writing, he tries to read, explore small towns, or ride his cool ebike, but mostly he just fetches treats for the dogs. He self-published his first novel, Kindred Feather, *in 2023.*

THE DELAWARE HOTEL

CORINNE JOY BROWN

FUNNY THING ABOUT a minin' town—first you get the miners, then the claim jumpers, then the speculators and the swindlers, and then, a swarm of squatters. 'Afore you know it, you got a boom town with everythin' anybody could want and some things you don't. You got your dry goods, a livery, a laundry, a depot, and on almost every single corner, a saloon with pretty dance hall girls right upstairs. Yes sir, all kinds of pretty girls.

Here in Leadville when gold was first discovered back in '60, our little no-name junction sprung up almost overnight and drew every kind of stranger you could think of. At least that's how it seemed, and I know 'cause I watched it happen right under my nose.

Me? I'm just a hardscrabble gold panner workin' with my pa, lookin' for traces of glitter in the muddy Arkansas. That big river's been good to an army of gold seekers. We're pretty sure there's still plenty of nuggets left from when the big strike hit. It ain't much of a livin', but once in a while, we get lucky.

The silver boom took over when the gold ran out. The strike of

'87. That was the big one. Upper California Gulch. More silver than anybody ever imagined. Week after week, all kind o' folks flocked over Mosquito Pass like they were on the road to heaven, and that ain't no easy trip. More'n one wagon tumbled off that steep trail. More like the road to hell.

But back to those saloon gals. They were the real deal—professionals. I heard they got their trainin' in Denver and Georgetown, another minin' camp up near Guanella Pass. Not that they needed trainin' so much, it's the business end they had to learn, and they did. They took care of the miners in Blackhawk and Central City too, where the gold rush first started in Colorado. The madam up there, Miss Silks, Mattie they called her, she's famous 'round these parts. She started a cash business and took it all over with gals of every description willing to make a miner happy in return for some pocket change. Some serious pocket change. But those gals had rules. Customers had to pay in advance, whether they were satisfied or not. Old Mattie ended up in Denver, "having providing a service to the city." That's what the papers said when she died. Anyway, I'm thinkin' that's how Miss Mary Coffey, a legend here in Leadville, got to town, but I can't really be too sure.

SOME SAID MARY didn't know right from wrong, or that she couldn't be controlled. I like to think of her that way—tough, not afraid of anyone. To this day though, it's said that she haunts the halls of the big, fancy hotel here in the middle of town, but conditions gotta' be just right—sometime after midnight, no moon, and the sky as black as pitch, or she doesn't show up at all. Then, when she does, the halls of that hotel turn cold as ice, lights flicker, and every dog in town howls like a banshee, worse even than a coyote, yippin' and cryin' and carryin' on. You can hear 'em all the way up into these hills.

WHEN MARY COFFEY got shot in the back by her husband, it sure took everybody by surprise. No one thought Lou Coffey had it in him, shootin' his own wife like that. I know I didn't. He always seemed to me to be a fair guy, though I didn't know him all that well. Could'a been the jealous type, 'cause Mary—she was a real looker—know what I mean?

Myself, I wouldn't stay in that hotel if you paid me. I'm not up for meetin' some ghost in a hallway like some say they've done. That's the God's truth. "Like the shadow of a woman," one man said, "hoverin' over the window near the stairs, or above them front doors like she was wishin' she could get out."

Some say a hotel ghost is a permanent resident. I wouldn't know. I never met one and I sure don't want to. But if that's true, Miss Mary might be the reason behind the decline of that establishment. That and the wrong name! Whoever heard of buildin' a hotel west of the Mississippi in the heart of the Rockies and calling it The Delaware? Somebody got turned around, I guess. Should have called it The Leadville. Now that would have made more sense.

But back when it opened in '86, it was the place to stay if you had the money, what with the mines coughing up silver like there was no tomorrow. Plenty of customers with fat wallets and fancy clothes could stay there, easy. Men like Mr. James Joseph Brown and his fancy wife, Margaret—Molly to her friends. They were society people, you know. Or the Tabors. You must have heard of them. His wife, Augusta—she sure could put on airs.

Miss Mary Coffey ran the "Frillery," a nice little "bo-tique" on the first floor of the hotel where she sold hats and gloves for the ladies and stick pins for a man's cravat. She had nice smellin' perfumes, too, that she said were from France and metal-tipped walking canes for the gentlemen. She sold fancy unmentionables as well, but I tried not to look too close at those.

You wonderin' how I know all this?

It's cause I got me a side job pickin' up deliveries from the post office and bringin' 'em to her door once a week. Hell, I was only eighteen. She needed the help and I needed the money. She paid me every time like clockwork. Plus, she'd give me that purty smile of hers and sometimes a nip from her brandy flask. I didn't mind that at all. No, I didn't.

"Imported," she always said. "The good stuff."

Didn't mind when she kissed me once, neither. I never told nobody, but I never forgot it.

I NOTICED MARY was good at helpin' a fella find the right gift for a lady friend, if he had one. She knew how to run that business real smart, better than her husband who was some kind o' no-account, work-wise. Never could hold a decent job. But Mary could sweet talk a sale better 'n most, and make a man feel good about givin' her his money. Maybe too good.

I first heard about what happened after my last delivery, seeing as how a shootin' was front page news, 'specially a woman. Some say Mary Coffee had it comin' to her. I don't know 'bout that. But my pa knew Lou Coffey real well and said he was quick to blow. I bet the man didn't think twice about what he done once he got his dander up.

Newspapers played it real big, like Lou was the devil himself. Damn if he didn't shoot her right there in their hotel room and wasn't ashamed to admit it. Folks heard the gunshot, called the sheriff, and Marshall Duggan arrested Coffey on the scene. Duggan wrote down what Coffey said. "...that he'd do it again if he got the chance."

Now, if that's not the devil, I don't know what is. I figured he'd be going to hell anyway for what he done. Mary didn't deserve that bullet, I'm sure she didn't. In fact, I told Lou Coffey once what a nice lady she was, but I'm not sure he took it right. I didn't like the way he looked at me, not then, or the very last time when I brought her parcels over. He was there, standin' at the door.

"What are you doin' here?" he asked.

"Just doing my job," I said. It was all I could think of.

"Your job? Well, get the hell out," was his answer. I left as fast as I could.

Poor Mary went to St. Vincent's for treatment but there wasn't much they could do. She never did walk again. The Delaware Hotel shuttered the shop and hung a closed sign in the window. Her customers weren't none too happy, but that was it. No one else could take over.

Mary ended up in a wheelchair, looked after by some nurses who managed a rest home down on the flats. I heard Lou Coffey never came to see her. I wasn't surprised. He had no remorse, none at all. I brought her flowers once, just to be kind. She sure seemed grateful and thanked me in a soft voice, but she didn't talk too much that day and didn't smile much neither. I guess she couldn't find a reason to smile. She wasn't the Mary I remembered.

I heard that Mary Coffey passed a few years later. The obituary said "died of natural causes." Ha! I had to read that one twice. That's hardly the way I would have described it, no, not at all.

TIME PASSED AND Leadville's last silver boom went bust like they always do. We went back to bein' a mountain town pretty much out of the way for most folks and just where we needed to be for the rest, a few miles from the prettiest lake you ever saw, the color of a robin's egg in morning light. The fishin's good and there's always plenty of game. Hunters and fishermen don't make us rich, but they don't hurt neither. Leadville might struggle sometimes, but still has a nice bunch of folks who carry on and support each other. I heard a new kind of miner is coming soon, lookin' for ore needed for the steel trade.

The Delaware hasn't been the same since the boom days ended either. Gone downhill in spite of all its fancy fixins' and trappins'. No more chandeliers in the lobby or bellmen to pick up your satchels. You gotta carry 'em upstairs by yourself. By the looks of things, the old traditions are gone, but believe it or not, I hear Mary's still around. Could be a rumor, but strangers aren't apt to lie. Some folks who stayed there just last week checked out in the middle of the night—scared to death they were seeing Mary floatin' above the stairs. "She had no legs," said one guest, "just half a woman hoverin' over 'em in the dark."

I'VE OFTEN WONDERED if it was me caused that son-of-a-bitch to do what he done. I'd like not to think about it, but it do creep up now and then. I sure liked that Mary and can't forget how sweet she was to me... but maybe, with someone else, too?

Just last night, the darkest night of the month, I was out with the mule in the barn, puttin' away some gear and old Nellie's ears perked straight up. "What's that, girl?" I asked, pattin' her on the neck. That mule's been a godsend all these years—best pack animal we ever had. Nothin' gets past her.

I listened hard and that's when I heard it, loud n' clear, a sound so mournful it sent chills up my spine. All of a sudden, Miss Mary come into my thoughts again, and a mournful feelin' washed over me like a cold rain. Tears filled both my eyes. I guess I'll never get over Mary Coffey and that's all there is to it.

Oh, and that sound that Nellie and me heard?

It was them dogs, from one end of Leadville to the other, howlin' at the top of their lungs, into the dark and moonless night, like Satan himself was on their tails.

—Colorado author Corinne Joy Brown is the author of ten books in print ranging from pop-culture non-fiction to award-winning Western and frontier fiction, to middle grade novels and colorful workbooks for kids about art and horses. She is currently agented by AKA Literary (Terrie Wolf) with new historical fiction in the works. Corinne is also the editor of a bi-annual journal that serves an international academic and secular research group, collected by the libraries of several major universities and the Library of Congress.

Corinne freelances for several magazines like Northwest Horse Source, Cowboys & Indians *and* Western Art & Architecture, *focused on the Western lifestyle, interior design, and art and architecture. She is also her husband's business partner in an upscale European contemporary home furnishings gallery established in 1976. They live in Englewood, Colorado with their German Shepherd and have one son and a granddaughter who already wants to be a cowgirl.*

What an Unbranded Cow Has Cost by Frederic Remington

THE SECRET TO CATCHING A BANDIT

KYLEIGH McCLOUD

A FIGURE CROUCHED down behind an outcrop near Twin Lakes junction and leaned forward for a better view of the road. Goosebumps prickled across his arms. Any minute now, the Leadville coach would be coming. Heart thundering in his ears, the deafening noise matched the Arkansas River's steady roar. Thanks to the sheriff, treasure awaited them.

The afternoon stagecoach appeared like usual in the distance. Frozen ground crunched beneath his feet as he stalked beside the rounded rocks near the road. With a deft tug, the bandana settled into place. As the stage approached, a quick-draw with thumb on the hammer, he peeked out and waited. When the coach reached the boulders, the bandit cocked the six-shooter and stepped out from his hiding place. He shouted at the stagecoach to stop and fired in the air, the shot reverberated in the mountain valley.

The six-horse team halted, and the lead horses reared. As the driver fought to rein in the belligerent horses, the guard reached for his rifle.

"Don't think about it," the bandit snapped, aiming at the younger man. The guard flinched. When the guard raised his hands, the thief bellowed, "Give me the silver and all your passengers' valuables. You do that, and no one will get hurt."

"Silver? Ain't no silver on this stagecoach," the guard sneered.

The bandit fired, the shot missing the guard. He cocked the hammer again and yelled, "Don't lie to me. I know there's a silver shipment on this here stage."

"All right. It's in the boot." The guard climbed down the stage and paused, glancing at his gun. He snatched up the rifle and aimed, but the bandit beat him to the draw. His body slumped over and fell to the ground with a thud, rifle sliding away from him.

Shrill screams pierced through the coach's canvas windows, and the stage lurched forward. The driver clenched the reins and fought to regain control of the team.

"Be quiet," the bandit admonished in a stern voice. He stormed the coach and yanked the door open, brandishing the six-shooter at the three passengers inside. An older woman with two young ladies gaped at the intruder. The thief waved the gun again. "Hand over your valuables, and be quick about it."

"Please don't shoot us," the eldest stuttered as she struggled to unclasp a necklace while the younger women continued to gawk. She removed the necklace and gestured at them to do the same. "My daughters and I will do whatever you want."

After he collected the women's valuables, the bandit glanced at the driver and headed for the back of the stagecoach. He uncovered the boot and searched through the luggage for their silver. A rock skittered across the ground. His heart sped up, and he leaned out just enough to study the side of the coach.

The driver fired, narrowly missing. Without hesitation, the thief returned fire. A groan came, and the bandit emerged from behind the coach amid the women's screams. "Silence!" The driver lay on the ground, reaching for the rifle alongside. Crimson staining the snow, another shot silenced the man.

A curse slipped out as the bandit holstered his six-shooter. He sprinted for the back of the coach and jumped into the boot, almost falling as the horses started. The thief winced at the mud pellets' assault. With a grunt, he hurried and pushed the luggage off the stage to the rocky ground.

The coach gathered speed, and the thief hustled to get the rest of the luggage off. He wasn't leaving without that damn silver. When they reached the last one, the bandit wedged between the coach and trunk and heaved. Upon landing in the road, the trunk lid broke and silver spilled out.

As the horses galloped, the stagecoach jarred harder over the bumpy road and swayed perilously. The bandit leapt, landing on the snow-covered ground and rolling to a stop. Not moving, he panted and pulled down their bandana. He sucked in several breaths and then rose. The women's distant cries faded as the thief hastened back to Twin Lakes Junction. Reaching the boulders, his face contorted at the sight of the two dead men. The driver and guard should have listened.

The bandit fetched his Appaloosa and pack mule from the Douglas firs near the riverbank. Someone was bound to hear the women's distressed screams and might stumble upon the scene. The thief gathered the silver and loaded it into their saddlebags, then fled.

A LITANY OF curses escaped from Sheriff Kirkham as he examined the carnage left behind. He removed his hat and clutched it wearily. The bandit struck again, and this time had murdered two men while nearly killing three women in a runaway stagecoach. How had the thief learned about the change in shipment time? He stared at the dead that had spoken with him mere hours ago until they blurred.

An empty trunk lay on the ground with a broken lid still attached to a lock. Kirk placed his hat back on his head and kneeled down, pressing a finger alongside the many horse tracks on the stage road.

Footsteps approached from behind and stopped. Kirk glanced up and discovered the footsteps belonged to Deputy Ames. "Sheriff? Did you want to talk to the three ladies that survived the ordeal?"

"Have the women recovered from their hysterics enough to answer some questions?"

His deputy shrugged. "They're lucky they made it out of that stage alive, which is more than I can say for some of the horses."

Kirk stared ahead at the rutted road and nodded, his gaze traveling to the bodies. He rose and brushed the mud and ice off his pants. "Get someone to help you bring Al and Johnny's bodies back to Leadville."

"You're riding to Granite?"

"I reckon there's not much the women can add to our investigation, being the bandit covered his face with a bandana. But I'll go talk with them, anyway." The sheriff sighed. He walked where his stallion Shooter waited and climbed into the saddle, gripping the reins.

"Want me to tell Jane not to wait on you tonight?"

"Please. When I get back tomorrow night, we're to meet. I'm more than convinced someone is tipping our thief off on the dates and times of the silver shipments, and we need to figure out who it is, as few are privy to these details." Kirk narrowed his eyes at the young deputy. Perhaps he was the leak? He tugged at the reins and headed toward Granite to interview the surviving passengers.

IN GRANITE, KIRK stopped at the livery and stabled his horse for the night. He walked over to the clinic he had passed along the way and knocked on the door. A dark-haired man answered and offered him a hand.

"You must be Sheriff Kirkham. I'm Doctor Preston Junior Taylor, but call me Taylor."

"Sheriff Kelly Kirkham. Most people call me Kirk." The two men exchanged a handshake. Kirk gazed past the lanky man and searched for signs of his witnesses. He heard nothing, which seemed unusual. "Are the three women here that jumped from the runaway stage?"

"They're resting. But I'll take you upstairs where the missus is attending to them."

Kirk followed the doctor, his nose twitching at the astringent aroma that cloyed the air inside the clinic. He lowered his voice. "Were any of them hurt?"

"Just bruises and scrapes." Taylor led him down a hallway and stopped at the room at the end. He rapped softly and cracked open the door. "Missus Whitmore, its Doctor Taylor. The sheriff is here and would like to speak with you about what happened today."

"Come in."

Taylor opened the door, revealing a disheveled woman with several bruises and cuts on her face. He stepped aside, and Kirk entered. The woman tried to fix her hair and grimaced, dropping her hands onto her lap. She offered a weak smile.

"Missus Whitmore…." Kirk lifted a nearby chair and set it in front of her, sitting. "You've been through a terrible ordeal, and I hate bothering you with this. But can you describe the man who robbed the stagecoach? Anything would help, even if you didn't see his face."

"I remember being surprised at his voice. It didn't sound like the voice of a man, maybe closer to a teenager going through the change? The way he spoke made me think of my youngest son."

Kirk nodded. "What else can you tell me about him?"

"His eyes ... they were so beautiful, especially with his dark, long eyelashes. They were a soft brown color."

The two continued to talk for another fifteen minutes, and when they finished, Kirk interviewed her daughters. As he did, his mind churned about Mrs. Whitmore's observations. He never suspected the bandit being a teenage boy. If the thief was, then he and his deputies needed to think of who else might know their shipment plans.

BY THE TIME Kirk reached Leadville, twilight decorated the horizon with ribbons of oranges fading into pinks. Fresh lumber permeated the air, and hammers clanged with each strike as Kirk maneuvered through the crowded streets lined with wooden skeletal frames of new hotels, saloons, restaurants, and shops. The discovery of silver had blown the town population sky high, and along with the boom, increased crime forced him to hire more deputies. Perhaps his newest hires weren't as trustworthy as he thought.

As Kirk rode near the station, he passed Deputy Ames outside and gave him a quick nod. He continued riding toward home, the sunset outlining the snow-capped peaks. Jane deserved to know he was back before he returned to the case.

Kirk arrived home and tended to his horse in the stable. After feeding and watering Shooter, he leaned heavily against the stall gate watching his horse eat. He tried to recall if any of his new deputies had a son that might fit the thief's description.

A hand on his arm startled him. "I'm sorry, it's me. I called for you several times, but you never answered."

"The highwayman struck again yesterday, only this time he killed the driver and the guard. And in the process, he spooked the horses and nearly killed the three passengers."

"Oh, my...."

Kirk kissed Jane's cheek and wrapped an arm around her waist. He nudged her forward, and they headed for the small house. "But I don't have time to tell you about the latest robbery. I need to meet with my men and fill them in on my interviews with the witnesses last night."

When they got inside, Kirk released his wife and noticed a picnic basket sitting on the dining table. He met Jane's gaze, and she smiled. "Deputy Ames warned me today might be long for you, so I packed cold fried chicken and a few other things. There's also extra food for your deputies."

"Thanks. The others will appreciate it, as I don't plan on letting anyone go home until one of them confesses."

Jane treaded to the table and brought the basket to him. "Should I expect you tomorrow?"

"Probably." Kirk shrugged. He took the basket and kissed her, then departed for the office. The walk would do him good after riding all day.

Kirk walked the muddied streets in Leadville and passed the two-story Healy house, admiring the majestic clapboard home. He wished he could give Jane a house like that. The basket swung as he hastened toward the station.

As Kirk approached the building, the muffled, raucous voices of his deputies carried outside. He entered, and they quieted. Their gazes dropped to the basket he held. Kirk grinned and moved the basket side to side, his deputies' eyes following it. He lowered the basket.

"Yes, Jane sent extra food along, since she knows what a ravenous bunch you are."

The men laughed. Kirk joined them and weaved through the deputies in the lanterns' flickering glow. When he reached his tidy desk, Ames patted him on the back. "You've got a good woman there, Sheriff."

"She has to be, to put up with the likes of you rowdy bunch." Kirk set the basket on his desk and uncovered their bounty of food. He set aside his supper plate of cold fried chicken and handed Ames the basket for them to pass around the room. "As you all know, the bandit learned the silver was to be transported yesterday rather than today."

"What are you saying? You think one of us is robbing the stagecoach?" Ames asked, his light brown eyes widening. The others muttered in agreement and exchanged glances.

"The thought hadn't crossed my mind ..." Kirk gave a heavy sigh. "Until yesterday."

"How could you not trust us, your own men?" Ames headed to the pot-bellied stove and poured a cup of coffee. He blew on his mug, steam dancing above. The deputy's gaze met the sheriff's. "We told you no one else knows about when the silver was being shipped out. Maybe it's you leaking the information."

Kirk slammed a fist on the desk, rattling his plate. "Someone is flapping their lips to our bandit unintentional or intentionally. And that thief must be a teenage boy according to one of the witnesses."

"A teenage boy?" Ames shook his head. "I doubt a kid could do this on his own."

A SMIRK SPREAD across the bandit's face as the sheriff and deputies argued amongst themselves. They glanced about and leaned closer into the building's shadows. The men's voices grew louder in their heated debate about the thief's age.

Fools. He shook his head. The sheriff noticed no one following him to the jail. They see me without really seeing me. I can do anything just like them, including robbing a stage by myself.

The bandit tamped a foot against the ground and waited for them to stop arguing.

Hurry it up. I need the next shipment date and time.

The sheriff and his deputies usually had the shipments every two days—except for yesterday's schedule change. Their shipment pattern had grown predictable, and the sheriff was too stupid to figure out he was the leak. When the sheriff blamed his deputies again, the bandit stifled a chuckle. The person they wanted was right under their noses.

Everyone takes me for granted. None of them would ever suspect me.

Deputy Ames snapped at his boss, "I'm telling you, no one has talked to any teenage boy."

They wouldn't be making the next shipment plans tonight, for they were too busy blaming each other. The bandit retreated, stomach fluttering in anticipation. *Whenever the sheriff and deputies plan the next shipment, I'll be there listening.*

One more. I just need one more shipment.

FOOTSTEPS THUMPED ACROSS the room. Kirk jerked awake and found he had fallen asleep with his head on the desk. He eased open his top desk drawer and withdrew a revolver, then rose sharply and aimed. His wife halted, her soft brown eyes widening. She stuttered, "Kirk, it's me."

"I'm sorry." Kirk lowered his six-shooter. He laid the gun beside his holster on the desk and stretched. "I guess I forgot to lock up after the deputies stormed out last night."

"Stormed out?"

Kirk rolled his neck from side to side. He should have gone home after his men left and cooled off. Jane closed the distance and stared at him, her hands going to her hips. She puckered her lips. Kirk swallowed. His wife was angry. He clasped his hands over hers and tugged them free. "It doesn't matter. Let's go home and eat breakfast."

"You're never home." Jane snatched her hands away. "And you never talk to me."

"How about I take the day off and let my deputies handle things around here? We could do whatever you want."

"Truly? You'd spend a day with me?"

"I—"

The door opened and shut, and Ames walked toward them. He smiled at Jane. "Sheriff, Horace Tabor wants to know when the next shipment will be, and what you aim to do about the bandit."

"Does this need to be decided today?" Kirk glanced at his wife, who had grown rigid. "I promised Jane I'd spend time with her today."

"I'm afraid, sir, if you don't… you won't be the sheriff no more."

Kirk gave a heavy sigh and rubbed his bleary eyes. They still had no leads on suspects other than a teenage boy. His stomach rumbled. He put on his holster and secured the six-shooter at his side. "I need breakfast to think, and then I'll talk with Horace."

"And you'll apprise me on the conversation later?"

"I will." Kirk placed a hand on Jane's back and nudged her forward. "Shall we go home and eat breakfast?"

As they walked home, his wife remained quiet while he replied to people's salutations. They neared the Silver Dollar Saloon, and he stared at the business longingly. Between the case and his wife, he could use a drink. Someone called his name, and Kirk turned toward the voice, discovering it was Horace.

"Stop," Kirk said to his wife.

The businessman approached them and introduced himself to Jane, then spoke to him.

"Deputy Ames informed me you still haven't solved the case. I need to get a shipment out as soon as possible and know it'll reach Buena Vista." Horace adjusted his hat and smoothed the front of his three-piece suit. He slipped his hand into a pocket and removed a watch, looking at the time. "I expect you in my office within the hour."

"Sir, with respect, I'm going home first to enjoy a nice breakfast with my wife. When I'm finished, I'll be there." Kirk gestured Jane to continue. A teenage boy walked past them, bumping into the sheriff. Kirk stifled a gasp and squinted as the boy fled.

"What are you looking at?" his wife asked.

"That teenage boy that passed us... I wondered if he was listening to our conversation. A witness thought the bandit might be a teenage boy rather than a grown man."

"What made her think that?"

"The way the thief's voice cracked when he talked made her think of her own teenage son back home, I guess." Kirk shrugged. They shuffled along down the busy street, when he spoke what was on his mind. "I don't know. She could be wrong."

KIRK WANDERED ALONG the storefronts and halted in front of a dressmaker's shop, passersby going around him. His gaze traveled over the dresses in the window. Their presence sparked an idea of how he could catch the bandit. The bell tinkled as he entered the store. A slim woman rose from her chair and set aside the purple dress she was sewing. "How can I help you, Sheriff?"

"I was wondering, do you have any ready-made dresses for a large woman?" Kirk stepped forward and fingered a golden fawn colored dress on the mannequin. The color would pair well with his wife's eyes.

"Are you looking for a dress for your wife?"

"Yes." Kirk clamped his tongue between his teeth at the lie. He could never afford to let Jane buy dresses from here. A silent shudder rippled through him. She would be livid with him, if she knew he was buying a dress for himself.

THE STAGECOACH JOSTLED over the bumps and divots in the road until Kirk's heart threatened to burst. If the bandit didn't attack them before the stage reached Buena Vista, he might jump out. He fidgeted with the strings on the reticule he had stolen from Jane. No one knew his whereabouts, not even his wife. His plan to catch the thief had to work.

As Kirk shifted positions in his seat, voluminous skirts mangled around his legs and further restrained him. He muttered a silent curse. How women could do anything in dresses was beyond him. If his deputies learned he had dressed as a woman and didn't catch the bandit, they'd never let him forget his failure. He shifted again and again while trying to untangle the excessive fabric. The stagecoach hit another bump, causing his elbow to jab the older man beside him. He forced an apologetic smile.

Shouts came from ahead, followed by a gunshot. The driver hollered at the six-horse team, and the stagecoach halted, almost jerking the passengers out of their seats. A gruff voice shouted outside, "Hand over the silver, and no one gets hurt."

Kirk fumbled with opening the drawstring purse, when the door banged open. The barrel of a gun eased through the doorway. He slid a hand inside the reticule and withdrew his six-shooter. The other passengers gasped as he tucked the revolver into the folds of his skirts.

A slim man leaned inside the coach and demanded everyone give him their valuables. Like witnesses had stated before, the bandit wore a bandana to cover his face. Kirk peered into familiar soft brown eyes.

Indistinct voices and rustling fabrics swirled about Kirk as he blinked. Those eyes. He pursed his lips trying to recall who they belonged to. Someone he knew? The other passengers handed over their valuables and pleaded with the highwayman not to shoot them. The bandit aimed his revolver at him.

"Your purse, too," the thief snapped. He cocked the hammer and squinted as if examining him. The bandit's eyes widened, and he released a surprised yip that jolted the sheriff out of his stupor.

Kirk snatched up his six-shooter and aimed. "Drop it!"

The bandit fled. Kirk rose sharply and staggered toward the door, ordering the man to stop. He fired on the ground next to the thief and repeated his order. The highwayman skidded to a stop.

"Put down the gun, and put your arms out to the side." When the man didn't comply, Kirk repeated his instructions. His hands trembled, and he readjusted his grip.

His back still toward the stagecoach, the thief dropped his six-shooter on the ice-crusted ground and extended his arms out to the side. Kirk's stomach churned. He forced himself to speak in an even tone. "Turn around slowly."

The bandit faced him, and they stared at each other. Kirk's heartbeat drummed against his ears. Who could have betrayed him with his inside knowledge of the silver shipments? Deputy Ames was too tall to be the thief. Perhaps Mrs. Whitmore was right, and the bandit was a mere teenage boy. He gestured at the man to remove his bandana and reveal his face.

This was it. He would learn the highwayman's identity at last.

When the thief shook his head, he bellowed, "Show me your face!"

The thief whirled around and sprinted toward the boulders. Kirk screamed at him to stop. Yet, the man continued to run. He sighted in on his target and fired, the man collapsing facedown onto the ground.

After he de-cocked his gun, Kirk gathered up his skirts and carefully descended from the stagecoach. He released his skirts and aimed his revolver at the listless body, easing toward it. As he approached, the man appeared to be dead. His barrel still aimed, Kirk kneeled beside him and checked for breathing. No breaths could be felt.

A heavy sigh escaped him. Kirk laid his six-shooter down and rolled the body over with a grunt. A blood pool surrounded the exit hole in the bandit's duster. He reached for the bandana and gave a hard swallow. His heart raced at finally revealing the elusive thief.

Kirk tugged down the bandana, and a hard sob choked him. He leaned over the body and embraced his dead wife.

—North Dakota Native Kyleigh McCloud lives in Minnesota with her husband and rescue cat. Writing has always been in her blood. As a result, she attended Minnesota State University Moorhead and graduated with a BS in Mass Communications, emphasis in Print Journalism.

While Kyleigh loves to read a variety of genres, her favorite is historical romance. She has always felt drawn to the 1800s time period. The Little House on the Prairie *series introduced her to this era when she was in fifth grade. Ever since, Kyleigh has admired the people's tenacity to survive back then. She and her husband love traveling the Midwest to visit historical sites.*

Aside from writing westerns, Kyleigh writes contemporary women's fiction and historical. She has multiple short stories published in various anthologies and also has two holiday novellas. To follow Kyleigh's writing journey, check her website www.kyleighmccloud.com, or follow her at www.facebook.com/authorkyleighmccloud.

On the Plains by Herman W. Hansen

ETERNAL FIRES

ROBERT J. McCONNELL

PEE-WEE WAS THE only one who seemed bothered by the evil things they'd done at the Matchless Mine earlier that day. He was so preoccupied with feelings of guilt that evening that he couldn't concentrate on the poker game. Finally, he had to quit. Haze said it was too cold to play, anyway, even though the four of them were huddled close to their large campfire.

Button gathered the scattered cards and stuffed the deck into his pocket. Pee-wee couldn't tell how Button felt about what they'd done. He was a pleasant companion, but hard to read because he was so colourless—a steady, faithful, listless follower with little individuality and no ambition.

Haze, on the other hand, was definitely memorable. He always wore fancy clothes and that damned English hat he'd brought with him from Liverpool. Pee-wee admired him because he was so polite and formal and consistently used big words that made some people feel inferior to him—likely on purpose. Haze had been staring into the campfire a lot that night and Pee-wee knew what the Englishman was thinking. He'd been doing the same thing himself—remembering and regretting.

After the gold mines petered out in '59, Pee-wee left Pike's Peak and drifted to Denver where he met Button and Haze. Then Thornton and Snort joined them, and they followed Thornton to Leadville in search of a more prosperous life. But all they experienced was miserable poverty. Then last night they found Dutch-courage in a bottle of stolen whiskey and Thornton told them that Horace Tabor kept lots of cash on hand at his Matchless Mine. He assured them it would be an easy take. So this morning, still drunk, they raided the mine, and Pee-wee's life took an irreversible turn for the worse.

"Thornton should 'a stayed with us, you know," Button said to no one in particular.

"Yeah," Snort said. "I like it when he's around."

"I do not anticipate that he will re-join us any time soon," Haze said in his haughty way. "We have all enjoyed the many attractions found in the lively taverns of Leadville—none more than our illustrious leader."

Pee-wee didn't give a shit about Thornton or the attractions of Leadville. Not anymore. He turned his attention back to the flames and his regrets. Deep down, he knew he was damned to Hell for eternity.

After a minute, Button stood up. "I gotta take a piss."

Haze stood too. "I too feel the need to relieve myself," he said.

The pair shuffled into the dark, leaving Pee-wee alone with Snort. Shit. He hated Snort. He couldn't stand travelling with the squat, ugly, vicious, half-witted prick day after day. The others despised him too, even Thornton. But they also secretly feared him. Stories circulated about what he'd done to men who'd crossed him. Women too. For a while, Pee-wee thought it was just so much talk. Half-truths at best. But they'd all witnessed what he did today at the Matchless Mine. The lunatic had descended into a frenzy, first with his fists and boots, and then with his knife. Admittedly, they'd all been drinking and had gone a little crazy. But nothing like Snort. None of them had the stomach to do what he did, not even Thornton.

After what he'd witnessed this morning, Pee-wee had to believe every horror story that he'd ever heard about the fat asshole.

Pee-wee had killed one of the miners—just one—and he'd done it with two shots. Ever since, he'd been trying to convince himself that shooting just one man wasn't such an evil thing to do. And shooting him twice showed he was merciful. Surely that was in his favour. And he'd raped one of the women. But that was all.

Afterwards, when they'd set fire to the buildings and flames were roaring towards Heaven, they sat around in a sort of stupor to watch. The miners had some good whiskey on hand, so Snort took a bottle out to a nearby stump. He looked completely satisfied with himself and drank non-stop until he passed out and fell over.

Snort interrupted his train of thought by dragging several dead branches close by and dropped a few onto the fire. Pee-wee welcomed the heat on such a cold night, and the flames were hungry.

"I gotta piss, too," Snort said, lumbering into the dark after them.

Now Pee-wee was free to contemplate this morning's unforgivable sins without interruption. The others had begun shooting people randomly, so he did too. He had no motive. He did it just because he could. He re-imagined the scene, over and over—firing point-blank, killing an innocent stranger. The man's death had been neither as swift nor as merciful as he wanted to remember it. His first shot had—.

A violent scuffling noise came from the direction the three men had taken. Pee-wee grabbed his six-gun and lurched towards the noise.

Beyond the first bushes, the glow from the campfire provided him with just enough light to see Haze and Button. They were sprawled on the ground with great holes blown into their chests and their blood flowing onto the frozen ground. But Snort was in one of his frenzies, wildly stomping and kicking someone on the ground.

Twice Pee-wee tried to shove him away. When that failed, he grabbed him by his coat and yanked him backwards. "Stop it, you dumb prick!"

Snort yanked himself free and resumed his brutal attack. So Pee-wee pistol-whipped the son-of-a-bitch on the side of the head. That got his attention and he reeled away towards the light of the campfire. Pee-wee held his weapon ready in case the bugger came back at him. If he even looked like he wanted revenge, Pee-wee would have gladly put a couple of slugs in him. Snort, however, kept moving towards the fire, so Pee-wee holstered his six-gun. Then he picked the fallen man up by the legs and dragged him out of the bushes and into the light of the campfire. Fortunately, he was still conscious and breathing.

"Snort!" Pee-wee yelled. "This's that crazy Irishman, Mat Duggan! You got the goddam marshal!"

Snort came back, holding his hand against the side of his head. The blow had calmed him down considerably. He bent over to examine the man's bloody face and then he looked at Pee-wee. "He ought not t' have killed Button," he announced solemnly.

"But how'd he do it?" Pee-wee asked. "They sure took a couple o' big slugs, but I didn't see no shotgun an' I didn't hear no shots."

"I dunno," Snort replied. But his ugly face broke into a wide grin. "But he got 'em both real good, didn't he?"

Pee-wee didn't bother replying. He removed the man's six-gun and great bloody knife. Snort watched him for a moment and then started back to the bushes. "Gonna get Button."

"Leave him. This bastard might not be alone."

Pee-wee only said that because he knew he'd puke if he saw Button again, all bloody and dead. He'd already heaved at the mine that morning, and he hated retching almost as much as he hated vomiting itself. "Gotta keep an eye on this bastard," he said. He returned to his place near the fire for a drink. He wondered how he missed hearing two shotgun blasts.

Snort hesitated, unable to decide what to do. Several times looked towards the bushes and then back at Pee-wee. Finally, he returned to the fire, flopped onto his bedroll, and gulped down some whiskey.

Pee-wee muttered curses at Duggan. How the hell could he kill both men with a shotgun that made no noise? And he'd been damned quick. Got both men before either one could make a noise or get a single shot off. Then he cursed Snort. The freak should be the one lying out there in the dark, all bloody and dead.

When Pee-wee began to feel cold again, he got up and threw several branches onto the fire. He watched how eagerly the flames licked the wood. They were like the fires of Hell—that's where they were all going. Face-to-face with Satan.

Sleep was impossible now, not with Button and Haze lying out there in the bushes. And Snort might have a change of heart and pistol-whip him in retaliation. Pee-wee figured if he was going to stay up all night, he may as well get shit-faced. He took another drink and then another. This was good whiskey. Not the rotgut that traders sold to the Indians. He held up his bottle and studied the flames of the campfire through the amber-coloured liquid. It looked kind of pretty. He'd think about Satan and Hell and eternal damnation another day.

"What'll we do with him?" Snort asked. Duggan had turned onto his side and had curled himself into a ball.

Pee-wee studied Snort. Even in the poor light he could see that the whole side of his fat face was burning red, and his ear had swollen hideously. That must hurt like hell, but the asshole was too stupid to notice. And he was too stupid to wonder about two shotgun blasts that made no noise.

"Nothin'," he said. "T'morra you better ride int' Leadville, see if you can find Thornton. He'll be in one o' the whorehouses."

Snort thought about that. Then he slowly got to his feet and lumbered back to the marshal. He stared down at the beaten man for a few seconds and shoved him with his boot. Duggan groaned.

"Leave him be," Pee-wee said.

"Might not be Duggan," Snort mused.

"It is," Pee-Wee said with weary indifference.

"Don't see no badge."

"So what?" Pee-wee didn't care who the bugger was. He got what was coming to him—sneaking around at night like that.

Snort bent closer to examine the man's bloody face. "But suppose he ain't Duggan."

"Course he is, you fat prick."

Snort returned to the warmth of the fire, his bedroll, and his whiskey. "Thornton promised t' give ten bucks to whoever got him, didn't he?" Pee-wee didn't reply. "He did, didn't he?"

"You heard him," Pee-wee said.

"So even if that fella's dead, he'll still pay me, right?"

Pee-Wee's smile was nasty. "You're thinkin' again, ain't you?"

"Sure," Snort said. "I think lots. So… is he gonna?"

"Mebbe."

"But what if he ain't Duggan?"

Pee-wee sighed. He decided to ignore the dumb question.

A minute of silence passed while Snort waited for an answer. Then he said, "You gonna sit up all night?"

"Mebbe."

"Wanna play cards?"

"Piss off."

Pee-Wee concentrated on the pulsing red and white heat at the base of the fire. Snort had earned his bragging rights, and of course Thornton would pay him. Why wouldn't he? After a while, Pee-wee leaned back. No stars tonight. Rain was coming. Shit. He liked clear nights because he could watch for shooting stars. Someone told him that seeing one was a sign of good luck. But what if it really meant bad luck? What if it really meant someone was going to die?

"Is he still breathin'?" Snort asked.

"Look for yourself—an' then check on the horses."

Snort got up and examined the motionless figure. Then he wandered into the dark without a comment, so Pee-wee presumed the man was still breathing.

The fire wasn't giving off as much heat as before. Pee-wee cursed Snort for not keeping it going. Luckily, the pile of branches lay close enough for him to reach by crawling on his hands and knees. He dragged several of them onto the fire. For a minute he watched the hungry flames grow into a roaring blaze and he enjoyed its heat. But the heat became too great, and he had to move back. Then it grew hotter and then even hotter.

Damn, but that fire was hot! He pulled all their bedrolls several feet further away.

Where the hell had Snort gone? He probably couldn't find the horses in the dark. Stupid shit. Pee-wee looked in that direction as if he'd be able to see beyond the nearest bushes. He sighed. He'd have to go himself. Pee-Wee struggled to his feet and stood still till the world quit moving. He was glad to get away from the heat. He took another gulp of whiskey, re-corked the bottle, and dropped it onto his bedroll. Then he staggered towards the horses. He hated lurching around in the dark. And he hated Snort.

Hell, he hated everybody.

Pee-wee had only taken a dozen steps when Snort emerged from the dark. "Find 'em all right?" he asked.

But Snort was looking past him. "Who the hell's that?"

Pee-Wee turned around and a wave of unimaginable terror swept through him. Between them and the fire stood the black silhouette of an elongated, unnaturally thin figure. He might have been a statue.

Nevertheless, Snort hustled forwards. "Hey! I got Duggan!"

The figure neither spoke nor moved. A tongue of red fire burst from the middle of the silhouette. A silent blow struck the centre of Snort's body and blew him off his feet. It left a huge, bloody hole in the centre of his chest.

Pee-wee panicked. He didn't know if he should run or draw his six-gun. A moment later he saw another tongue of red fire and a silent blast smacked into the side of his chest, spun him around, and slammed him to the ground.

Pee-wee had never experienced such pain. He never dreamed such pain existed. He started screaming. He was still screaming while the black form glided closer to watch him die.

—Robert McConnell is a retired teacher who lives in Calgary, Alberta. He was first introduced to cowboy fiction through the early television series, but especially by Gunsmoke, Roy Rogers, *and* Lash Larue. *Through all the following years, he never lost interest in the cowboy culture, past and present, and he never missed watching good western movies,* Dances with Wolves *and the* Lonesome Dove *series. He has spent much of his time visiting the historic Bar-U ranch and talking to experts who give talks about the old west and welcome questions from visitors. Since retiring, he has writ-*

ten two full-length western novels, unfortunately still unpublished, as well as a number of short stories, a stage play, and a radio play. In preparation before writing any western fiction, he has spent many hours doing detailed research into the history and geography of the old west as well as the cowboy lifestyle, famous and infamous cowboys, and horses and cattle.

When the Land Belonged to God by Charles Marion Russell

LEADVILLE: A PICK, A PAN, AND CHOPSTICKS

P.A. O'NEIL

WILTON EVERS STEPPED down from the Wells Fargo stage onto the surprisingly cosmopolitan streets of Leadville, Colorado. Evers was there to finalize the contract for the railroad spur planned to join Leadville's valley with the rest of the United States. Up until then, silver ore, people, and goods had to be transported by wagon to the closest railway depot, some sixty or so miles from town, delaying people's progress by a couple of days. Mine owners anticipated transportation of the ore by rail would less likely be waylaid by bandits.

"Here's your bag, mister," shouted the driver as he removed Evers's carpetbag from the back of the stage storage area.

Evers tipped his hat before taking the bag. "Thanks. Can you tell me the way to The Cortez Hotel?"

"Yeah, it's around the corner, half a block, that way." The driver pointed past his team of horses. "Hey, and when you get there, tell May Lee, I'll drop by for dinner later and she better have my usual dish available." He said with a drawl and winked.

Wilton Evers nodded before stepping off the brick cobbled street onto a boardwalk facing more brick structures several stories taller than wooden ones. As he walked the direction he was given, he tipped his bowler to the women he passed on the way, until he was finally standing beneath a large sign which read The Cortez Hotel.

The building was made of red brick trimmed in sandstone. He opened the doors of mostly glass panes and was surprised by the tinkle of a little bell which sounded with each direction of the door. There was no one behind the front desk. Setting down his bag, he was about to tap on the little cap bell sitting along the registration log when a handsome woman of indiscriminate age walked in from a side room. She was dressed in the fashion of the day which made him feel as though he might have just as well been in Philadelphia or Chicago.

"May I help you?" Her voice was soft yet slightly accented.

Evers gulped before he replied, "Uh, yes. My name is Wilton Evers and I have a reservation."

She nodded as she turned the register around for him to sign. "Yes, Mister Evers. We have been expecting you."

To Evers's ears, she pronounced his name as, *"Meester* Evers." He signed the register but as he went to pick up his bag, she gestured for him to stop.

She turned her head to her left and cried out, "Diego!"

A teenage boy dressed in a porter's uniform came from around the corner. *"Sí, Señorita* Cortez?"

"Lleve las maletas del señor Evers *a la habitación* 314." The *"senorita"* reached into a pigeonholed shelf to withdraw a key.

"Sí, Señorita." The porter nodded, took the key, and gave a slight bow to Evers as he picked up the carpetbag and departed up the stairs.

Evers watched the boy, turned back to the woman, and then back to the boy before asking, "Uh, where is he going?"

"He's taking your bag up to room 314. It faces the front of the building. You should have an excellent view of the town."

"Yes, yes, I should have guessed. Thank you, *Señorita...?*"

"Cortez. I own this hotel, as well as the adjoining restaurant."

"Yes, thank you, *Señorita.*"

"Miss Cortez will be fine."

He nodded again, replaced his bowler and headed for the stairs. With his foot on the first step, he turned back. "Oh, the stagecoach driver wanted me to give someone a message."

She had moved from around the desk and was heading into what looked like the restaurant. "Yes, what is it?"

"He wanted me to tell May Lee, he would be here for dinner and was expecting his favorite dish."

The woman chuckled. "That must be Travis. Thank you, sir, the message has been received."

"Oh, your name is May Lee?"

"Yes, Mister Evers. Actually, it is Mai Ling, but most people shorten it to May Lee. It's Chinese." She continued to the restaurant without looking back.

Wilton Evers mumbled to himself as he absently took each step up the stairs, "Mai Ling Cortez?"

Just as the hotel owner had promised, the view from Room 314 carried most of Main Street with evergreen covered mountains in the distance. He unpacked his few belongings, hanging up his extra shirt after placing his shaving cup and razor on the mirrored dresser. Wilton's stomach growled, so he pulled his pocket watch from the pocket on his vest to see it indeed was nearing time for lunch.

Before reaching the final step to the first floor, Milton observed a middle-aged couple come through the front door. Their destination the hotel restaurant. "Ah, Miss May Lee, I hope we're not too early for our reservation?" asked the gentleman. His hat in one hand and his other on the lady's elbow, he guided the woman in as they followed Miss Cortez.

Wilton overheard her gentle, sing-song voice as she led them deeper into the restaurant. "Not at all, you and Missus Addams are right on time. In fact, I have your favorite table saved as you requested."

From the hotel foyer, he watched as she pulled the chair out for the lady before being replaced by the man, Mr. Addams presumably, to push it back in with her on it. Miss Cortez then pulled back his chair. She informed them of the special of the day and introduced them to a young blonde woman who had walked up beside them, explaining she would serve as their waitress. Miss Cortez's smile was genuine as she approached Wilton. "Mister Evers, is there something I can do for you?"

"Yes, ma'am. The enticing smell from your kitchen wafted up to my room. Do I need a reservation to eat in your restaurant?"

"Not at all. I always have tables reserved for hotel guests. If you will follow me."

Wilton noticed the sound of a silk petticoat gracing the floor as she spun. He followed her into the seating portion of the restaurant, taking stock of her size and shape. Mai Ling Cortez was small in stature, but broader in the back than what he would expect of a Chinese woman. Her coal black hair was sleek and fixed into a thick braid which wound around her head and held in place with a cloisonne comb above the back of her neck. She led him to a section of tables closer to the kitchen entrance than where the Addams's sat. At another table, two young women were chatting, with an occasional giggle coming from one or the other.

She left him with a smile and before long the same girl who had attended the Addams's was at his table, handing him a menu. "Welcome to The Cortez. Today's special is Honey Chicken or Carne Asada. All dishes come with the appropriate rice and beans upon request. May I get you something to drink while you peruse the menu?"

"Just black coffee, thank you." She turned, but stopped when Wilton asked, "There is an extreme variety of foods on this menu, how come?"

The girl nodded and smiled. "I get asked that all the time. Miss Cortez believes the restaurant should reflect her style. I'll be back with your coffee."

When she returned, he placed his order for the Honey Chicken, then sat back and watched the restaurant fill up with other patrons looking for what he believed would be an interesting lunch. He hadn't long to wait for first his coffee and then later his lunch. Miss Cortez was still sitting guests, but his server had been joined by a Negro girl who also took orders and a Mexican looking teen who efficiently cleared the tables after each set of guests left. Each of the young ladies wore matching pinafores starched to perfection.

Several pieces of golden fried white meat, covered in a sweet, crystalized honey glaze and sesame seeds was delivered before he finished his coffee. On the side, was a plate of fried rice with peas and carrot chunks, which smelled as enticing as the chicken. A surprise plate with a fried egg roll was the last thing the girl set down. "Would you like a pair of chopsticks, or would the knife and fork suffice?"

Wilton raised an eyebrow and smiled. "Chopsticks would be great. Thank you."

She reached into a deep pocket of her apron, and after laying them on the table, she said, "I'll be back with more coffee."

He was surprised by the delicious flavor and tender texture of the chicken. The rest of the meal was just as tasty, and the egg roll filled with seasoned cabbage and sprouts, made for an excellent finish. He took his time as he ate, watching the staff move smoothly throughout the restaurant like bees going back and forth, to and from the hive. He noticed others had ordered the same as he, while others chose the Carne Asada. One elderly man was served a bowl of beans and a basket of tortillas. It truly was an interesting restaurant.

He ate slowly as he watched the diners come and go. When the restaurant was mostly empty, he caught the eye of the owner.

"Mister Evers, did the meal meet with your satisfaction?"

He sat up as he pulled a cloth napkin out of his shirt collar. Expanding his chest while patting his stomach, he commented, "Yes, Miss Cortez, it certainly did." She chuckled and went to move on, but stopped when he asked, "Since things seem to have quieted down, I was wondering if you would join me in a cup of coffee, or maybe tea even?"

She stopped one of the servers as she passed. "Would you bring a fresh pot of coffee and another cup to this table?" When she turned back, she found Wilton standing with his hand outstretched, palm up as he gestured to the other chair. A sly smile appeared as she withdrew the chair and gathered her skirt, only to find he had come around the table to gently push in the chair for her to sit. "Thank you, Mister Evers," she commented once he took his own seat. "Why do I feel you have something you wish to discuss?"

Wilton blushed. "Is it that obvious?"

"It's not often I am joined by a man with such charming manners. Even by my few admirers here in Leadville."

Chuckling, he replied, "Well, that is indeed a shame." The waitress returned with a pot of coffee, a trivet, and a clean cup.

"No, Sonja, the extra cup is for me."

"Sorry, Miss Cortez." The girl dipped her head and hurried back into the kitchen.

Once more alone, Wilton added, "What I meant was, a successful woman as yourself is always deserving of respect."

Pouring coffee for them both, Mai Ling nodded and gave a tight-lipped smile.

"Miss Cortez, please call me Wilton. I am here representing the conglomerate wanting to run a railroad spur from Leadville to the east-west line between San Francisco and Denver."

She sipped from her steaming cup. "Well, Wilton, we already have regular stage service provided by Wells Fargo and a union of teamsters who take the ore out of the city and bring other goods back from the rail junction. Wouldn't what you propose put them out of business?" She flashed a smile. "And you may call me, Mai Ling."

"Well, yes, Mai Ling, but I thought talking with someone who really knew Leadville might help me with my presentation. Who, other than yourself, would seem to know the people and their attitudes? You seem to be well liked by your customers and staff."

"Thank you, Wilton. I've worked hard to earn their respect and my reputation as a fair and successful businesswoman."

Wilton set down his near-empty cup. "Maybe we could start with a little information about yourself. I mean, how did you get your start in Leadville? Did you always plan to open a hotel and an adjoining restaurant?"

Mai Ling picked up the pot and refilled his cup without asking. "My story begins long before coming to Leadville. As you might have guessed, I am of mixed heritage, Spanish and Chinese. My father was a ship's captain who married the daughter of a merchant he dealt with in Hong Kong." She topped off her own cup and set down the pot. "When I came along, my mother insisted we have a permanent home. I grew up in San Francisco. Papa purchased more ships while Mama grew bored keeping house, so she opened a restaurant in Chinatown, The Blue Lotus."

Wilton's head picked up. "I've eaten at The Blue Lotus. It is indeed a fine restaurant. I can see where your management skills were derived. Did you come to Leadville to open a branch restaurant?"

"No, I ended up here for the most foolish of reasons."

Wilton set down his cup with an obvious click. "Oh, I can't imagine you ever being a fool at anything."

Mai Ling looked down and smiled. "Well, that's what my mother called it when I told her I was in love with the boy next door." She looked up and past Wilton's head and continued in almost a dreamlike state as her voice softened. "Gold had been discovered during the Pikes Peak Gold Rush. The miners put down roots in what they called Oro City. My betrothed was going to seek his fortune, our fortune is what he actually said, when he left San Francisco for Colorado. Being impatient..."

"Impatient, that's another thing I can't imagine of you."

"Well, I was," she chuckled. "After a few weeks, an argument with my mother found me on a stage east. What I didn't know was the gold strike had played out and had been replaced with silver-filled lead. Oro City had been replaced by Leadville when I arrived, and it was not much more than scattered shacks and tents. I found my true love wasting the afternoon in Madame Dianna's oversized tent with one of her doves. Of course, I made quite the scene, demanding he reimburse me the cost of my passage."

"Right there on the spot?"

Mai Ling's smile grew wider than before. "Yup, boy did I make a scene, too. He emptied his pockets, and I walked out, never to see him again."

By this time, Wilton was chuckling with her. "Now, I do believe I could see you doing that. Do you mind if I smoke?" He pulled a silver case from a breast pocket and offered the contents to her. She held up her palm before he removed a professionally rolled cigarette from within. He patted his pockets for matches, but when he looked up, she had removed the glass globe from the table lamp and was offering up the bare flame. "Okay, so you were almost stuck in a backwater town in the Rocky Mountains. It still doesn't explain how both you, and Leadville, became today's success."

"Pride, Mister Evers..."

"Wilton, remember?"

"Yes, Wilton—sheer pride. I wasn't about to place my sore back into a stagecoach to California, only to dwell on my mother's repeated, 'I told you so.'" Wilton chuckled again at her candor before she continued. "I now had some money in my pocket and when I looked around for a decent place to eat, I found there just wasn't any."

"So, you opened your own restaurant."

"Well, you could call it that considering most all of the businesses were set up in tents and shacks. I found an abandoned shack, grabbed it before anyone else, and from the few provisions I purchased from the trading post I started cooking. Beans and tortillas mainly. The smell of good cooking brought the hungry miners in looking for a meal."

"What did you charge for your simple fare?" he asked.

"Nothing."

Wilton's eyes grew wide as he sat up straight. "Nothing?"

"Nope. I told them for every miner the first meal was free. Afterwards. they would have to pay for the delicious food."

"That was a bold move, Mai Ling." Wilton slowly shook his head as he reached for his cigarette case.

Mai Ling tipped her head and leaned forward, as she softly spoke, "You know what was even bolder?"

He shook his head, cigarette between his lips, as he reached for the oil lamp.

"I made them wash their hands at the door."

Wilton Evers dropped the unlit cigarette from his gaping mouth. The oil lamp in his hand was still approaching his face.

"Wilton! Watch out for the flame," she alerted.

Wilton put the lamp down and picked the cigarette off the table. He blushed and huffed as he shook his head. "Well, yes. I guess I wasn't looking." He carefully lit the cigarette, taking a long draw as he regained his composure. "And did the men do as you asked? Wash up, I mean."

Mai Ling covered her broad smile with her hand as she tried not to giggle. "If they wanted to be fed, they did."

They were both laughing now when one of the servers came from the kitchen. "Miss Cortez, sorry to interrupt, but all the tables have been set for the evening meals. Is there anything else you would like for us to do?"

Still smiling, Mai Ling shook her head. "That's all, for now. You girls head on back to the kitchen for your own meal." The girl curtsied and turned away. "Now, Wilton, where were we?"

"You were telling me about your first meals served here in Leadville." He flicked the ashes into a little glass dish before gesturing with a swoop towards the tables. "A bold move, for sure, but evidently it was successful enough for you to open this place."

"It took many years to move up to a place of this quality. The miners wanted good, hot food at a reasonable price, and I gave them what they wanted. I moved to a finer built wooden structure in about a year's time, which happened to coincide with the mining engineers and speculators moving into town. When they discovered how rich the silver vein was, it attracted more miners and teamsters, who saw a chance to set down roots. Pretty soon, other businesses arrived to serve the community. There was a dry goods shop or two, a dressmaker for the wives and daughters, a doctor, a school, banks, and even a couple of different churches established. Not necessarily in that order, mind you."

He stubbed out the cigarette. "You make it sound all neat and pretty, Mai Ling."

"Well, just because east moved west, it doesn't mean that the west moved out." She poured the last of the coffee into her cup after offering him some.

"I don't get what you mean."

"Madame Dianna and her likes didn't just disappear. The gambling houses and saloons simply moved to one side of the town, while the god-fearing folk lived on the other. If I wanted to move up to a different class of clientele, I had to move with them. When I saw a chance to purchase this block, I took out a loan and built The Cortez Hotel and Restaurant, hoping one would pay for the running of the other."

"That 'other side' of Leadville, it's what I was expecting when I stepped off the stage."

Mai Ling nodded. "Oh, yes, don't let this gentrification and brickwork façade fool you. Leadville had its wild cowboy past. Have you ever heard of Doc Holliday? Well, he shot and killed a man just a few blocks from here."

"Doc Holliday," Wilton exclaimed. "Did you see him do it?"

She shook her head. "No, but plenty of others did. Enough willing to testify it was in self-defense."

"You used the term, 'gentrification,' what exactly do you mean."

"I mean when the East Coast money moved to Leadville, they brought with them their way of life." With an elbow leaning on the table, she gestured pointedly with every comment. "Thanks to them, we have brick houses, paved streets, and underground water systems. Did you know there are plans in the works to lay a sewer system, eliminating the need for everyone's outhouses? It gets mighty cold here in the winter. People have been known to die of exposure by heading out to relieve themselves in the middle of the night." She slammed her palm on the table causing him to sit upright.

"East Coast money, you say."

"Yes, when the mining surveyors reported back to the conglomerates, claims were staked, and an influx of money came to make improvements to the mines. If one played their cards right, a miner, an engineer, or even a teamster, laid down an investment into the various mines and made their fortunes, small and large."

"And were you fortunate enough to get in on the ground floor of these investments?"

Again, she leaned forward for her soft words to be better heard, "I made a point of listening to my customers as they talked over dinner."

"You eavesdropped?"

Mai Ling placed her hand flat on her chest as she sat up straight. "Oh, heavens no! But I can't help it how loud some men talk between forkfuls."

Wilton's mouth dropped open, then closed, then opened again. He burst out laughing and was pleased to see she was laughing as well. Their jocularity was interrupted by Sonja as she approached the table and stopped.

Mai Ling dabbed the corner of her eye with the extra napkin from the table. "Yes, Sonja, what is it?"

"Cook wanted to let you know Missus Brown was here with young Larry with a basket of mudpuppies."

"Please tell Cook to put them in fresh water and place them in the ice cooler. If one of you girls would like to make a little extra money, you can help him clean them tomorrow morning before your shift begins."

Sonja curtsied and turned to leave, but her mistress held out her hand to stop her. "Oh, and Sonja, would you ask Missus Brown to come in here please? Tell her I have someone I want her to meet."

"Yes, Miss Cortez."

Wilton was replacing the handkerchief he had pulled from his pocket after wiping his own tears from laughing. "Mudpuppies? What are those?"

"They are like freshwater shrimp. Larry Brown occasionally brings us a bucket a couple of times a month. Under his mother's supervision, he earns a fee by the pound."

"Well, that certainly sounds like an excellent way to help supplement the family's resources."

"Oh, his family's resources need no supplements. No, his mother married up and she wants her son to understand what it means to have your own funds and not to take his father's money for granted."

"Sounds like a very levelheaded woman."

"Oh, yes, she is." Mai Ling tilted her head to look past him. "And here comes, Maggie Brown, now."

Wilton stood to greet the woman approaching the table. Maggie Brown was a small, yet sturdily built woman with a smile which lit up the room. She was wearing a split skirt of tan suede and boots. Mai Ling stood and embraced the woman, presenting her with a peck on either cheek.

Maggie Brown's voice was strong yet friendly. "One of your girls said there was someone I needed to meet."

"Missus Maggie Brown, this here is Mister Wilton Evers."

Wilton held out his hand expecting a polite gesture in return. What he got was a strong clasp, followed by a shake. "Pleased to meet you, Mister Evers. Any friend of Mai Ling's is a friend of mine."

"How do you do, Missus Brown? I'm not exactly a friend of Miss Cortez, yet, but I sure hope to be."

Mai Ling blushed. "Mister Evers is here to discuss the new railroad spur with the town council tomorrow."

"I thought that was all finalized."

"No, no, just the final decision as to how it will approach the town. I've been told there has been some disagreement as to where to lay the tracks." Wilton's smile faded. "Oh, how rude of me, would you care to sit down and join us, Missus Brown?"

"No, thank you, Mister Evers, I've got to be getting my son home to clean up before supper." The sound of the swinging door between the dining room and the kitchen caused them all to jump as it was swept open wide, hitting the wall behind. "Speak of the devil, here's my son now."

He was almost as tall as his mother, and his clothes were caked with dried mud. "Ma, Cookie paid me for today's catch. Can we go home now?"

Maggie placed her arm around his shoulders and pointed him back to the kitchen. "Son, get your muddy self out of this dining room before Miss Mai Ling has us both thrown out."

"It's all right, Maggie, I'll have one of the girls sweep it up." Mai Ling chuckled.

"That's awfully nice of you, Mai Ling, but Larry, you shouldn't just bust right in when adults are talking. Now, say you're sorry to Miss Mai Ling, and meet Mister Evers."

The boy dipped his head. "I'm sorry, Miss May Lee." He turned and held out a recently washed hand. "It's nice to meet you, Mister Evers."

Wilton shook the boy's hand. "The pleasure is mine, Master Brown."

"Master Brown?" Larry looked at his mother with a furrowed brow. "Did you hear him, Ma, he said, 'Master Brown'?"

"Well, son, that's the way people in England and New York address boys."

"Oh, I understand." He nodded then perked up. "Mister Evers, Ma wants to go to England. Says she wants to see the Queen."

Mai Ling turned away to chuckle behind her hand. Wilton's mouth dropped open as his eyes repeatedly blinked. Maggie gave her son a gentle push towards the kitchen. "Git! Nobody here is interested in Queen Victoria."

"Actually," offered Wilton, "she's not much to look at. She's old and rather fat."

Mai Ling started laughing again. Maggie put her hand on her hip. "That's no way to talk about a queen."

Wilton shrugged. "She's not *my* sovereign."

This started everyone laughing.

The tinkling of the bell above the front door pulled Mai Ling away from the table with an, "Excuse me."

Maggie and her son returned to the kitchen only to be replaced by one of the serving girls with a tray at her side. She approached Wilton's table. "Are you through with your coffee and such?"

"Yes, thank you. And please give me the bill for lunch and tell me where I am to pay."

"Oh, no bill. The Cortez Hotel runs like a room and board. The costs of your meals are included with the charge for your room."

He sat down alone at the now cleared table, hoping Mai Ling would have a chance to return. He watched as she seated a young couple at one of the tables alongside the windows. Though he couldn't hear exactly what she said, he did note her tone was friendly and warm. As she walked past him towards the kitchen, he held up a finger. "Mai Ling, will you be able to come back so we can finish our conversation?"

She only smiled as she passed towards the kitchen door. The girl known as Sonja walked out of the kitchen carrying menus. She was followed by her boss lady. "I've only a few minutes as the dinner crowd is beginning to arrive," Mai Ling said as she took her former seat.

"I see you're probably going to be busy. I just wanted to know why you spent time discussing Leadville—and yourself of course—with a complete stranger."

Mai Ling smiled. "Wilton, I was aware of your coming even before I received the wire for your reservation. You see, I am one of the inhabitants of Leadville who want to see it grow beyond the mines, the small businesses, the rich people's fancy houses, and the opera house the Tabor family had built. I want Leadville to grow to become a destination, not just a spot on the map."

"Very interesting, but what does that have to do with me?"

"Wilton, you represent the company that wants to bring in the railroad. I want you to take back not only a good opinion of Leadville but the feeling this is a place where others want to invest. The silver mines, though strong, can't last forever. They have to play out some time and Leadville should diversify if it wants to continue, and that begins with the railroad spur to the outside world." They rose as the bell tinkled again.

"Wait, one more thing. What makes you so invested in the future of Leadville?"

She turned back as she walked away. "Because it's what I am, an investor." She displayed her hands palms up. "How do you think I was able to afford all this?" She turned, giving her attention to the man, Wilton recognized as his stage driver.

"Travis, I got your message and your usual table is waiting, along with your favorite dish."

"Oh, May Lee, honey, you don't know how long I have been waiting to once again taste your fine cooking."

Wilton walked past the couple on his way out of the restaurant.

Mai Ling caught his eye but spoke to the other man, "Oh, I can only imagine, Travis. It's good to feel wanted."

—P.A. O'Neil's stories have been featured in over fifty anthologies, on-line journals, and magazines. She and her husband reside in Thurston County, Washington. Her collections, Witness Testimony and Other Tales, *as well as* Two Sides of the Same Coin, *are available on Amazon. She was the winner of the 2023 Mustang Flash Fiction Award with her story, "The Great Burro Revolt," which was also featured in* Saddlebag Dispatches *anthology,* West of Dodge. *Her article, "Northwest Passage," about the Ellensburg, Washington Rodeo from the Summer 2022 issue of* Saddlebag Dispatches *Magazine was a finalist for a 2023 Will Rogers Medallion Award. For links to books which feature her stories, please visit her Amazon author page: P.A. O'Neil.*

Mount Rainier by Albert Bierstadt

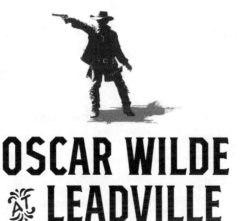

OSCAR WILDE AT LEADVILLE

RICKEY PITTMAN

LEADVILLE WAS AT the height of its economic prosperity when Oscar Wilde arrived in April of 1882. The Irish-born Wilde, at the age of twenty-eight, had already achieved international fame, recognition, and celebrity status as a poet, lecturer, and playwright. Leadville was one of the stops on his 1882 American Aesthetic Movement Lecture Tour across the American continent. As soon as Wilde stepped off the South Park train, a man in a brown Herringbone suit approached him.

"Mister Wilde?"

"Yes."

"I am Wallace, an employee of Mister Horace Tabor. I've been sent to pick up your trunk and take you to your room in the Clarendon Hotel. It is my honor to meet you. All of Leadville is looking forward to your lecture tomorrow night. Ah, here comes the conductor now with your trunk." Wallace tipped the conductor, picked up the trunk and said, "Shall we proceed to your room, Mister Wilde?"

After his trunk was deposited in his room, Wallace said, "Sir, would you like to take a stroll about town? Mister Tabor wants to meet you for drinks and treat you to a fine supper later this evening."

"Indeed, I would like to see more of Leadville and perhaps you can fill me in on some history."

As they walked, Oscar Wilde noted the many brothels, gambling halls, stores, hotels, and boarding houses. Outside one brothel, with a sign that read, Emma's House of Pleasure, he saw two women screaming and fist fighting.

"Do you see things like this often?" Wilde asked Wallace.

"Nearly every day. Sometimes the hurdy-gurdy girls fight with knives. I know those two. Probably fighting over a customer."

Wilde said, "I guess any mining town is going to have brothels."

When they passed a parlor house, a bell rang. Wallace said, "Hear that? That's the madam telling her ladies that customers have arrived. Leadville has grown so much because of the silver boom that we now have three red light districts and several hundred sporting girls. The more elegant live in the nice parlor houses like Mollie Mays, others live in smaller local brothels, or one-room cribs. The most desperate walk our streets. Many of our demimonde end up buried in our pauper cemetery. The miners are hungry for women, so all the cathouses and sporting women seem to get plenty of business, but as they say, you get what you pay for."

They passed an alley, cluttered with trash. "See that?" Warren said. "That's Stillborn Alley, where the whores dump dead babies." Across the street, Wilde saw two cursing, growling men who had drawn Bowie knives. Both of them were bloodied.

This really is the Wild West, Wilde thought, *but not much different from parts of London.*

Wallace said, "It is time for us to return to the Silver Dollar. Mister Tabor said he would meet us there."

As news of Wilde's arrival spread through town, the lobby of the Silver Dollar quickly filled with a crowd of men anxious to catch a glimpse of the famous celebrity who had fascinated, enraged, or shocked American newspapers and audiences. The curious Leadville citizens gathered around the saloon's bar and speculated on whether the star of the tomorrow night's lecture was the wildly dressed dandy they had heard of, a libertine who carried lilies and daisies.

The Silver Dollar was one of the town's sixty saloons. Miners, business owners and employees, and dancing girls flocked around Wilde at the mahogany and white oak bar, all eager to buy him drinks and ask questions about his tour and tomorrow night's lecture. Wilde, set his cane on the bar and posing with his boot on the foot rail, expressed his admiration for the beautiful decor of the Silver Dollar, especially the diamond dust mirror behind the bar.

The crowd parted as a man made his way to Wilde. He held out his hand, "Mister Wilde, I am Horace Tabor, and I am pleased to make your acquaintance. Would you care to join me at my table?"

"Certainly." Wilde excused himself from the admirers and followed Tabor to his table.

Tabor said, "Mister Wilde, I was delighted when your American agent, Miss Marbury, contacted me expressing your interest in visiting Leadville. She praised you highly."

"And what did Lizzie say about me?"

Wallace, his guide through Leadville brought them schooners of beer. Tabor dismissed his employee. "Thank you, Wallace." Looking at Wilde, he said, "Miss Marbury said you were eccentric, but a man of brilliant wit."

"Thank you, but sometimes my wit is half-armed."

"Mister Wilde,

Tabor chuckled and said, "Oscar, you are hardly a half-wit." He slid a rolled-up canvas across the table. "This is my gift to you, Oscar. It is a greater area map of Lake County and Leadville, drawn this year by Henry Wellge and published by Beck & Pauli Lithographing Company. In addition to Leadville's businesses on the map, you'll notice that near the Matchless Mine, I have penciled in this phrase, *The Oscar Lode,* a rich silver and tin vein which I have named in your honor."

"I am honored, Mister Tabor."

"By the way, Molly May, a lady friend of mine will soon join us for some conversation." He signaled Wallace to bring them more drinks. "I see her entering the saloon now."

When Molly May joined them at their table, the men removed their hats, stood and Tabor introduced her to Wilde. "Mister Wilde, may I introduce to you my friend, Molly May?"

When Molly extended her gloved hand, Wilde took it and said, "I'm very happy to make your acquaintance, Miss Molly."

"Thank you, Mister Wilde. I hope you will find time in your busy schedule to drop by my place. I have several female employees who will be delighted to meet such a handsome, refined and educated gentleman. Perhaps you can join me for tea?"

Wilde reflected on what he had heard and seen regarding the many brothels in Leadville. He felt an immediate attraction to this lady in a beautiful blue day dress, with a string of diamonds around her neck. "I should be able to arrange a short visit before my stage leaves the day after my performance."

Tabor said, "Before she moved to Leadville, Miss Molly was quite a celebrity in Cheyenne and Deadwood. She's a very influential citizen and quite popular in our community. She also has the only telephone in town in case you need to call anyone. You passed her lavish house and place of business on 5th Street as your stage entered the town. She is making money hand over fist."

"Miss Molly, what is one secret you can share with me that explains your financial success?" Wilde asked.

Tabor said with a wink, "She has a silent partner. Miss Molly has proven to be a good investment." He removed a thin sterling case from his vest, removed a cigarette, struck a Lucifer and lit it. He then slid the case to Wilde. "The cigarettes are rolled from fine Kentucky tobacco." After Miss Molly May left, Tabor said, "Do you miss Ireland or England, Mister Wilde?""

Wilde lit his own and inhaled deeply. "There are moments when I feel a bit homesick, but where I'd really like to be is in sunny Italy, where I can lie in my gondola, smoke cigarettes, and write poetry. Yet, I must admit that each place I've visited on this tour has given me inspiration and ideas to write about."

Tabor said, "Your agent said you are scheduled for several cities—Memphis, Canada, New England, and finally in New York and then back to England. Are there any stops you are especially looking forward to?"

"Yes, indeed. I've arranged to go from Memphis to New Orleans and Mobile, and from there to the Mississippi Gulf Coast where in June, I have an invitation to stay at Beauvoir, the home of Jefferson and Varina Davis. I'm told the name *Beauvoir* means beautiful view, and as I am known as the Apostle of Aestheticism, I am eager to see the beauty there. I've read President Davis's two-volume of *Rise and Fall of the Confederate Government* that was published last year. I admire Davis greatly and have followed his career carefully. He is the man I would most like to meet in the United States. I know it is not always easy to talk about your nation's war but I do know it took three million Union soldiers and four hard years to defeat the South. After an interview, I was told by the editor of the *Times Picayune* that I had sensible views of the Confederacy. Why do I think this? Well, the cause of the South was much like that of Ireland. The South fought their war seeking autonomy, self-government, and freedom from heavy taxes, just like the Irish have done in their wars. When I visit Beauvoir, I plan to present a signed photo of myself to the President and a signed book of my poetry to Missus Davis."

Tabor nodded. "Now, Mister Wilde, before you retire for the evening, are you ready to see my mine and view the miners at work?"

"Take me to your Irish, Mister Tabor. Can we bring a bottle of whiskey with us?"

THE NEXT AFTERNOON, after an interview with a reporter from the *Leadville Daily Herald* and a short rest to recover from Leadville's 10,000 feet above sea level altitude sickness, which the attending physician described as "light air," he made his way on the Clarendon's skywalk to the third floor of the Tabor Opera House, then to the theatre on the second floor. Before he stepped on the theatre's wooden stage, he sat for a moment on a black leather rocking chair to collect his thoughts for his lecture to the mining audience. When he strode to the stage, the six-foot Irishman in his dapper suit with shoulder-length hair was greeted warmly by the nearly 900-member audience. He tossed his cape over one shoulder, tipped his hat, and began.

"I am honored to be a speaker in this beautiful theatre located in Leadville, which I believe is the richest city in the world. And you hard rock miners and businessmen who have delivered tons of silver from the earth deserve credit for the prosperity and growth of Leadville. And speaking of silver, it is appropriate for me to begin my lecture on aesthetics—on artistic taste and talent, on art and beauty in life, by mentioning a sixteenth century Italian artist, a master silversmith

I discovered years ago. His name is Benvenuto Cellini. He had a special gift when he worked with silver—everything he created possessed an extraordinary, mystical beauty that caused him to receive honors and recognition from royalty and the papacy. I have seen many of his works in my travels. It is because of you providing the world with silver, that works of art like his can be created."

Wilde's lecture continued with many references to the art of the Greeks and of the Italian Renaissance and the art he had seen in his tour across America. He added, "I must say that Mister Tabor's fine theatre we sit in tonight is a wonderful example of what beautiful art should be. I understand that the solid brick walls of its three stories are sixteen inches thick. And there is so much in the ornate interior that draws the eyes, inviting contemplation—the beautifully painted walls, custom made stage curtains, the luxuriant carpets, and the first gas lights in Leadville, these sights will long be in my memory.

"Yesterday, I was lowered in darkness in a big bucket into the heart of Mister Tabor's very profitable Matchless Mine and honored by the newly named Oscar Lode. After we descended, I was delighted to share three rounds of whiskey with Irish miners. That short journey caused me to appreciate the hard work required to bring silver to light.

"I believe Leadville can be the center of a great Western renaissance, that there are artists here in this audience, who like Mister Tabor have a powerful, creative inner theatre, and can create art, and please the world!

"Now I must conclude this lecture, hoping I have opened some eyes to the need and beauty of art. After I conclude my tour, I must return to England. I will return with this unforgettable memory: In the Silver Dollar Saloon where earlier I had shared several drinks, I saw this sign over the piano: *PLEASE DO NOT SHOOT THE PIANIST. HE IS DOING HIS BEST.* As every man I've seen in Leadville is armed, and a man's revolver seems to be his book of etiquette, I see the wisdom of the notice. In application to myself I will borrow these words and say to this fine audience, *PLEASE DO NOT SHOOT TONGHT'S SPEAKER. HE HAS DONE HIS BEST.* Good citizens of Leadville, you businessmen, you miners—I wish you prosperity and I bid you goodnight."

The audience cheered and applauded. Wilde bowed dutifully, but as his eyes searched the audience, he saw three men on the front row holster their pistols.

—Rickey Pittman, the Bard of the South, is a storyteller, author, songwriter, and folksinger. This Dallas native was the Grand Prize Winner of the 1998 Ernest Hemingway Short Story Competition. Pittman presents his historical songs and stories presentations at schools, libraries, museums, and Celtic festivals throughout the South.

THE CLEANSING OF WOODBURY MANSION

LOUISE BUTLER

WATER STARTED POURING down the front steps of the Woodbury Mansion in the dark early hours of October 22. A cleft, V-shaped and barely half an inch wide, had opened on the top step of the front porch and was assumed to be the source of the cascade. It is certainly true that water spewed out of the cleft a full eight inches in the air before falling in a continuous, graceful arc down the ten steps from portico to ground. But closer examination showed that the dark water seemed to generate itself along the entire curve of the steps.

The volume of water was staggering. It gushed at an estimated 60 gallons per minute. Walking the steps was at first perilous and later impossible. But if the source of the water was a problem, its destination was a mystery. As the water reached the bottom of the steps and spread across the carefully kept lawn it neither gathered nor moved beyond the property line. Instead, it sank into the earth, leaving an oily froth on the saturated ground.

"It is as if the house is cleansing itself."

I spoke the words softly as I walked the perimeter of the property.

If so, it was long past due. I walked from the northwest corner of the iron-fenced enclosure of the Woodbury Mansion almost to its opposite corner, thinking that I knew this house in the same way that it knew me. I also knew I was going to have to enter the house today, whether I wanted to or not, and both I and the mansion knew that inevitability.

It was now 9:36 a.m. The police had called me as soon as the torrent had been detected. Workers from all the appropriate agencies were here, shaking their heads, talking in small groups, slurping coffee and looking generally confounded. Once more, the Woodbury Mansion was going to make the papers.

"Eunice. Eunice Woodbury." I turned to greet a man I had known when I lived in the Woodbury Mansion.

"Chet! It is good to see you." I waved off the policeman who started to intercept the reporter hustling across the road and ignoring the yellow tape designed to hold just such people at bay.

I gave Chet a quick hug, much to the irritation of the rest of the news personnel sequestered at shouting distance.

"You look great, Eunice. It has been too long."

"Only three years, Chet. I just moved back to town." I stopped to look at his ID badge from the *Denver Post.*

"It looks like you've got the job you always wanted, Chet. But are you sure that a questionable story about a water-main leak in North Denver is what you hoped for when you signed up for this job?"

"Not a water-main leak, lady." A worker from the water district was joining us and had heard my last comment.

"You're sure?" Chet asked in full-on reporter style.

"Absolutely."

Two policemen had now joined this conversation, as well as a member of the fire crew who had been called because—well—I guess because everyone had been called.

The water district supervisor looked at everyone and then pointed to his men standing around the manhole that each had exited some minutes before. "We've shut off the water to the entire house and grounds—a full city block, actually. It is making no difference in the water coming down that slope, and what is more, the water usage data for this area shows nothing—not a single gallon of loss. There wasn't any extraordinary water usage for this house, or this area, last night or in the past week, month or months. We don't know where that water is coming from, but it isn't the water main."

"Sewer?"

I don't know who asked that obvious question, but I knew what the answer was going to be.

"Nope. No odor, no flocculation, and I'll bet no contamination, though we are sending samples to the lab. On site checks for hazardous materials are all negative." He paused. "I'm certain that it isn't sewer."

We had been joined by the police supervisor. "So, what is your best guess?"

The men from water, sewer and fire each took turns.

"No guess."

"No idea."

"No answer."

I glanced at Chet in time to see him checking out my response as well. We both knew the Woodbury Mansion's capacity to confuse minds and confound the laws of physics.

"Officer—gentlemen—would it help if you got in the house to have a look around?" I made the offer in anticipation of their next question.

The fire chief interrupted the group's hesitant pause. "Is it safe?"

True, the mansion had been empty since I left Denver almost three years ago, but it had not been abandoned. Caretakers were there weekly. My sisters used the facility for family events, reunions, every holiday and group celebration. I had been there several times since my return. Indeed, the house and I had had a good long talk just two weeks ago.

The Woodbury was safe—depending on how you defined the word, at least.

"It is quite safe, I assure you. The house is used regularly by family members and, if this water has not damaged the interior, you will find it quite habitable."

"How will you get in?" Chet asked. "You can't get up the steps without danger of being swept away. Water weighs eight pounds per gallon. Rushing like that it packs a punch."

His answer came from the officer who had been first on the scene and had called in the problem.

"The side and back entrances are clear. The water has confined itself just to this main, southern entrance."

"Good," said the supervisor. "I'll get a small team together."

"Meet me at the north entrance." I said, moving toward the car I had hastily parked across from the distinctive south portico. "Chet, would you like to come, too?"

He was already moving with me. The question had been rhetorical.

As Chet slid into his Mustang, he gave me an almost apologetic look. "You know I'll have to include a brief history of the Woodbury in this article."

"And you know that a cascade of water that appears and disappears at will is not going to be the strangest story told about this place."

There was an awkward pause as I buzzed the car around to the smaller, less grandiose, north entrance to the mansion. The Woodbury is built on a hill and every drive, save the steep, straight steps to the imposing south entrance was built on a curve. The north service drive took us to the door a few minutes ahead of the contingent of men walking the perimeter to get to the north side.

"It's okay, Chet" I said, getting out of the car, "We all know the story. It's a good story. Just don't make this generation sound any stranger than we admittedly are."

We exchanged quick smiles and knew they sealed the bargain.

THE STORY OF the Woodbury Mansion was woven into the boom-and-bust history of the Queen City of the Plains. Like the people of the gold rush days, the Woodbury's tale was a combination of heroics, hysteria, facts and fabrication. They also involved my great-great grandfather, George Rische, who arrived in Denver in 1878 on his way to Leadville and the money that he thought was there for the taking. That is the same year H. A. W. Tabor, the great silver magnate of Colorado, was elected lieutenant governor of Colorado.

Tabor and his legendary second wife, Baby Doe, set the bar for Gilded Age excess, but his contribution to my family was in the form of a chance meeting between Tabor and George Rische. In that conversation in the bar of the Buckhorn Exchange Restaurant—which still exists, still serves up good meals and still hosts intimate and important conversations—Tabor expansively told George that the lasting money in boom towns was made by the men who outfitted the miners, not the miners themselves.

Rische took the advice and started a dry goods company which began the Rische fortune. His only child, a daughter named Helen, both inherited her father's fortune and married into a second one, a railroad family named Woodbury.

My great-grandfather, August Woodbury, was said to be a man who learned from every mistake he ever made, and he made a lot of mistakes. He was smart and successful. He assured his wife a comfortable life, increased the family fortunes and fathered first a daughter and then a son. It was shortly after their son's birth that Helen moved into a separate bedroom choosing to abandon her husband and devote herself solely to her children.

When August complained of the distance and absence of warm reception to each attempt at conjugal pleasure, he was informed by Helen that the "messy" portion of her life—and, by extension, his—was done. If this declaration led to anger, argument or ultimatum, there was no record of it.

From that time on, Helen's life turned steadily inward, centered on her children and moving in society only to perform those functions required for matrons of means. August's life, on the other hand, turned outward, becoming an active participant in every worthwhile organization in Denver.

August appeared to have led a virtuous life. There was never any scandal associated with him. There were neither rumors among the men, nor gossip among the women. In all things, Helen's husband, August, seemed to embody a civically, morally and ecclesiastically upright life. And then he died.

It was on October 22, a gray and weepy day, when August Woodbury was buried. His stern and stalwart wife, whom everyone said was "holding up" remarkably well, shepherded her children and friends through the funeral services and internment with much grace. She hosted a tasteful luncheon that included all the appropriate people. At around 4:30 in the afternoon, she thanked her guests for coming. The children were sent to a neighbor's house to allow Helen a quiet night. The servants were sent home, with the generous admonition that anything still needing done could wait until the 'morrow.

Alone in the house, Helen Rische Woodbury began her mission. She systematically went from one room to the next, one floor to the next, one wall, desk and cupboard to the next, removing every photo, painting and likeness of her deceased husband. She placed them in neat rows in front of the main fireplace. She then moved a generous hassock next to the fire, sat down and committed each painting and picture to the flames, cutting some to pieces before placing them on the pyre. Empty frames, some broken, some intact, formed a latticed pile on the carpet behind her. It made no difference if the precious pictures included her or her children, all were burned. Her shocked servants found her feeding the last of the pictures into the fireplace when they returned to their duties around 6:00 a.m. the next day.

Their concerned questions were met with a civil request for tea, followed by a morning that was typical by almost every definition. It was reported that she did take a nap in the afternoon which was both deeper and longer than usual. She never referred to or explained her actions.

Decades later, well into her 80's, Helen Woodbury died quietly and alone in her bed in the Woodbury. Three generations later, I knew for a fact that Helen had never left the mansion. Neither had her husband.

I was thinking of that commonly shared history as I walked up to the north door of the family mansion. The coincidental date of Great-grandfather's burial and today's deluge were not lost on me. I knew that my actions two weeks ago and the actions of Helen Woodbury long ago were certainly implicit in the cleansing action of the house today. It may also be why I would not be welcome in this house ever again. Nevertheless, I entered as I always had—respectfully.

I gently placed my left hand against the door, as if on the back of an old friend. I had done this before entering the Woodbury for as long as I could remember. When we came to live here after my grandfather's death I had placed my hand on the unopened front door the first time I approached it. The polished wood was a warm, exquisite swirl of caramel colors to my eye. When I touched it, it felt more than warm, it felt alive, even overjoyed with the light touch of a wonderous child. For some reason it had become a ritual. Sometimes it was an absent-minded brush, occasionally a playful, angry or frustrated slap, but I always announced my presence to the Woodbury, and it always responded.

My touch today was tentative, and the house answered with caution. Did I really want to come in? Today? Of all days?

With my right hand, I shook free the housekey, unlatched the dead bolt and unlocked the door. I was pushing it open just as the policemen and their retinue came into sight walking up the drive.

"Please, Chet, hold them here for a minute, then show them in. I'm going to get the lights on and have a quick look around." My face turned in toward the dark interior.

Chet immediately moved toward the group with his hand upheld to stop them.

"Gentlemen, you may not know the full history of the Woodbury..."

"Please," I whispered, stepping through the door, "let everything be good in here."

The north door entered what used to be a cloak room. The door to my right went into the study, left the informal dining room and beyond it to the kitchen and pantry. The center archway, now lacking a door of any kind, proceeded straight into the hallway. It was through this door that I walked, reaching for the hall light which would dispel the shadows from the massive central stair. The switch was sticky with a cold moisture. I knew she was here, waiting for me on the stairs.

Two weeks earlier I had crossed a line. She was angry and there was a reckoning coming. Putting it off only led to water pouring down the steps of the Woodbury. If she wanted this meeting, she would have it. Spurred by some gathering anger of my own, I walked up the stairs without a hesitant step toward the amorphous haze that became more distinct as I rose to the second floor.

I HAD BECOME aware of the presence of Helen Rische Woodbury in the home I shared with my family when I was still a child, shortly after we moved into the mansion. She was a feeling in the air, distant and occasionally disapproving, especially if we were loud or raucous. But the mansion itself also had a feeling, one which was always warm and welcoming. If one presence was chiding, the larger feeling of the home itself was comforting. The cold was fleeting but the warmth was ever-present. As I grew older, I came to understand that this house had a gender. The Woodbury Mansion was, without question, masculine—grandfatherly, protective and joyously warm. That is when I started searching for the history of my great-grandfather, August.

The more I learned the more I liked him. The newspapers were full of anecdotes relating to his life in Denver. He was a humorous man, a busy man, generous, involved in the community and frequently quoted while attending town socials, picnics and musical events. He played the tuba in the Masonic band. But not a picture could I find.

When I brought home a stack of books of Denver's history, several of which referenced the life and times of August Woodbury, I started feeling a tension between the house and the remnants of Helen that still wafted through the rooms. When I poured over a book about August, Helen would crowd the room with all the usual tricks of specters.

Most people who have experienced a ghost-like presence will talk about a cold, clamminess, or a scent of perfume, a low-pitched sound or an apparition of uncertain form. These are not part of the natural makeup of the spirit, but simply its way of trying to get our attention. They use our senses to manipulate us in a way that suits their purpose.

My great-grandfather's spirit occupied this house and seemed content to stay within its walls. It was as if he and the house were one, inseparable, encircling and protective. His aggrieved wife, Helen, on the other hand, roamed the house.

If the Woodbury Mansion whispered, *"Sleep well,"* Helen would add *"But lightly."*

Right now, Helen was not whispering at all. She was leading me on, up the stairs to the spacious second floor landing. Her form, expending energy that must have cost her every atomic particle of psychic energy she possessed would gather but then drift apart. The gray blur of her corporeal form would show a strong outline then dissolve into smoke. I had the strong sense that it took far too much energy for whatever was left of Helen to maintain a form.

Yet there she was again, hovering above the picture—*his* picture.

"Out."

It was a deep sound. Some might have thought it a moan of wind, but I heard the word distinctly.

"Out."

"It belongs here."

"O-o-o-out." This was more than a sound. It entered my very body and chilled to the bone. It was a threatening sound.

She attacked the painting of August Woodbury. She battered her amorphous self against the portrait to no effect. The effort caused her form to dissolve into ineffective wisps, and I warmed a tiny bit.

Here was the cause of the Mansion's cascade. Here was the need for its cleansing. I had not only found, but brought back to this house, an image of the one person Helen could not tolerate. Here was, at long last, a picture of August Woodbury.

While researching the history of the Rische and Woodbury families I had found an obscure reference to a small portrait of August Woodbury which had been gifted to H.A.W. Tabor's estate. The picture, not five inches square, had been put in a gilded frame that added another two inches on each side. I had found a black and white photo of the painting in a portfolio of the art of the Tabor estate.

On a hunch, I had sought permission to examine the stored art and artifacts of the Tabors. My work with the historical society earned me that privilege, and I was given access to a pallet of crates, boxes and one large barrel. I had barely started the second crate when I found it. The painting was wrapped in a linen cloth and almost fell out of the fabric into my hand. Here, at long last, was the face of my great-grandfather.

It had taken a slim ten days of negotiation to earn custody of the painting and another month to have it restored. Two weeks earlier, I had brought it to the Woodbury and carefully hung it on the landing between Helen's bedroom on the left and August's on the right.

The minute I brought the painting out of its brown paper wrappings I had felt the house tighten around me. There was a leap of happiness followed by a sense of acute fear. In the same instant the rush of that other presence, the roaming spirit of Helen Rische Woodbury, had exploded on the landing. There was a fury of movement so intense that it could coalesce in no direction and seemed to bounce from wall to wall.

Now, I found myself standing where I stood then. Repeating what I said then.

"This is great-grandfather's house as much as yours. He deserves to be here."

I had received no response that first day, only a fury of random movement. But now, Helen had had time to marshal her strength. She reformed. Ignoring the painting that would neither dissolve nor break, she turned her assault to me. Her choking vapor swirled around my head, blocking out both light and air.

"Out."

"He stays." I gasped.

"The house goes if he stays."

"Why?" I knew I was choking on her anger as much as the sullen vapor that settled closer with each exchange.

"Out."

"Why?"

I could feel the answer better than I could hear it. The fury of a hundred years pouring out like the water of the Woodbury.

"He wanted others." The word "others" trailed off in a hiss.

"A woman?"

"Any company other than my own."

The swirl that was all that was left of Helen left me for a moment, gathering in front of the painting. Her voice was small, and I strained to hear it. *"Sitting in his bath. Ignoring me as usual. Saying he was going out again to some meeting, some gathering, any place away from the parlor in his own home."*

I could hear the men downstairs and tried to call them up to the stairs, but no sound came. I was surrounded again by the anger of Helen Woodbury.

"People were already talking. Why was he constantly present around town, but never with his wife?

"He told me the truth that day. He would never dishonor me but planned to always avoid me. I would always be his wife, but never his companion. He said..."

There was an hysterical edge in her voice. A catch in the flow of sound. *"He got out of his bath. Taunting me. He looked at the grimy water going down the drain and said he had just washed me out of his life. Me. Me. His lawful wife. I was to be refused his attention and obedience simply because I refused his bed."* There was a pause. She gathered her last strength, pounded against the picture and gave a wail that seemed to split the house from top to bottom. *"Out."*

There was nothing else she could do. The vapor shattered like glass and rained down onto the floor, on me, and down the stairs to the men gathered at the bottom step.

They stared up at me as the shards of mist cascaded down the landing and sublimated from solid to gas at their feet.

Chet shook himself to action first. He leaped over the dispersing vapor and took the stairs two at a time.

"What was that? *Who* was that? What...?" He asked, taking my freezing hands in his.

I started to talk, but my throat seemed clogged with a dry heat. I just shook my head, then tried again to make some sound, to shed the feel of Helen's grip on my throat.

"She hates the water." I gasped. I glanced at the portrait of August Woodbury, at last hanging in his own house.

"She hates the water. The longer it flows, the cleaner the house gets. She leaves with the water."

Chet looked at me and then at the firemen, police and water officials busy convincing themselves that what they had seen had not really happened.

"Then we let it run, Eunice. The water runs until the house says it is enough."

I nodded, but my eyes were on those of August Woodbury, not on Chet.

WATER STOPPED POURING down the front steps of the Woodbury Mansion in the late afternoon on October 24. A cleft, V-shaped and barely half an inch wide, closed on the top step of the front porch. The cleft had been assumed to be the source of the cascade. In truth, the torrent of water had started over 100 years earlier when August Woodbury, a scorned husband, told his wife he had washed her out of his life.

The volume of water had been staggering, for the stains of anger, resentment and frustration are hard to wash away. But August Woodbury had cleansed his mansion.

—Louise Butler has most recently been published in Alien Dimensions, Metamorphosis Magazine, Cricket Magazine, *and* Chicken Soup for the Soul. *She was nominated for the Pushcart Prize by* Copperfield Review. *Butler specializes in historic fiction that is engaging and fanciful while seated in solid research. With a background in both science and economics Butler likes data as much as chocolate and, like chocolate, thinks data is better when sweetened with a little imagination. Louise uses her love of research to indulge the story-telling inheritance of her Sámi ancestors.*

TWO MILES HIGH

LEE CLINTON

EVIL NEVER LOOKS like the devil. It wears a disguise to stalk the vulnerable. By the time Margaret 'Maggie' Bray realised the danger, it was all too late. She had been trapped. Yet on that chilly day in January 1885, when the bright-eyed eighteen-year-old from San Francisco stepped off the Rio Grande to proclaim, "Leadville, here I am," all she felt was optimism.

"Everyone comes to Leadville," the porter had said, "but what brings you here, miss?"

She didn't answer. How could she possibly have told of her quest? She was in search of a rich husband, but best to keep that to herself.

It was a wise decision. She didn't find one. Well, at least not a rich one. The pickings were slim and the competition high.

While her natural beauty, youth, and trim figure were attractive, so were many others. Especially those professional beauties who had gravitated to that mining boomtown high in the Rocky Mountains. They knew how to play this game and could charm the gold leaf off a gilded statue. They also knew of timing and patience when husband hunting. The same two essential requirements when fishing. Unfortunately, they weren't of Maggie's temperament. She could be impatient and had never caught a fish in her life.

While suitors were plentiful, few had struck it rich. The opulent lifestyle Maggie had conjured up in her mind from fashionable lady's magazines like *Godey's,* were unfortunately, a grand delusion. Every now and again she did get close to netting a live one, only to have him snatched away by a beguiling smile or words of sweet nothing. "Phooey," became her refrain in response to this frustration, that eventually grew into annoyance, then bitterness, and finally resentment. After nearly a year on the hunt she had become desperate.

Then along came Jacob Palmer. He wasn't wealthy, but there was potential in his business, selling machine parts and lubricants. The other pressing reason for making her move was the fast-approaching winter. It could be bitterly cold in that place two miles high in the thin air of the Rockies. Maggie wanted to be warm, and free from feelings of loneliness and melancholy that were beginning to take their toll.

After introductions, at a Sunday church picnic to the lake, Jacob was encouraged to give his views on the importance of marriage, where he replied with a stumble, "Well, yes of course, every man will be in need of a wife at some point."

Maggie replied without hesitation, "Thank you Jacob. I graciously accept your proposal."

His bewilderment was swept away by a full embrace and a moist kiss. Jacob was bowled over, and Maggie had landed herself a fish, maybe not a prized catch, but nevertheless, one with prospects.

The wedding took place on Saturday May 8, 1886, and the Saint Mary bell of the Annunciation Church rang out. Happiness ever after was ready to follow, and how I wish I could report that it was so, but life knows no such certainty. Sometimes a turn of events from afar can intervene to collide with the best laid plans.

OF ALL THE lawless towns west of the Mississippi, Leadville was at the centre of the Wild West. What started as a tent city known as Oro, grew to 8,000 prospectors looking for gold, only to be picked clean of surface deposits by 1866. It had been boom-to-bust in just six years. Those few who did stay, discovered lead in the black sand and assay tests revealed that it could produce fifteen ounces of silver per ton. The boom had returned, and by 1880 it was home to 30,000 and had the new name of Leadville. The deposits deep below were immense, and mining was now on an industrial scale. Smelters worked twenty-four hours a day to melt the milled ore, and if the price of silver eased, the answer was to produce more.

With the wealth came the miners, engineers, and merchants, followed by the saloon owners, gamblers, prostitutes, charlatans, and the depraved. One of these was a man named Sean Kelly, a solid Irishman, tall in stature, with a mean disposition that had been honed by beatings from his violent father. When aged sixteen and approaching six foot, a clear two inches over the man who had taken the stick to him so many times, young Kelly stood up and announced, "Enough."

With eyes of rage, his father grabbed his *shillelagh* to deliver a thrashing. To protect himself, his son thrust out a forearm, landing an unintended blow to the bridge of the nose. The sight of blood that followed sparked fury in the young man, who seized the heavy gnarled shillelagh from his father to strike blow upon blow to the head. When his father fell to the floor, calling for mercy, he was met with the vengeance of his son's heavy work boots. Sean Kelly had chosen to end this once and for all.

Remorse should have followed from the realisation of what he had done. Forgiveness from the Lord would have come if only he had sought confession. Instead, he felt a sense of superiority and gratification. Evil had entered his soul. The devil had come calling, to dwell like a cancerous tumor.

To stay was to face the scaffold for murder most foul. So, he ran with his father's savings and some meager belongings all the way to America. In New York he learnt the way of the streets, while in constant fear of having his past discovered. He covered his tracks by lying about his origins and living in the shadows. He trusted no one, cheated on all and stole from those who offered the hand of sympathy. His impulse was to fight, and he took to carrying a shillelagh like his father had done. He told himself that every difficulty, no matter how big or small, could be solved with brute force. No one was safe, especially women. When his carnal advances were rejected, he took what he wanted, luring those unable to resist against his size and strength, to places where he could force himself upon them.

By the age of thirty he had morphed into a street beast of rat-cunning intellect that could hide his evil intent. He was of the gutter, living a life of continuous crime, violence, and depravity and with no way out.

Until...

When forcing entry into an East River warehouse, Kelly was surprised by what he thought was a nightwatchman. A blow to the side of the head rendered the man unconscious and no longer a threat. However, the opportunity to rob had been lost. When leaving the scene and almost as an afterthought, he searched his victim and found a leather satchel hidden under his coat. He took it and quickly stashed the valise under a floorboard in his boarding house, away from the prying eyes of others.

The following morning, the word was on the streets. A courier from the Five Points gang had been knocked over while carrying graft to Tammany Hall. The courier was sure he could identify his mugger and the gang had put up a handsome reward. Vigilantes were out on the streets like vultures, searching for the perpetrator to claim the prize.

Kelly wondered if the nightwatchman was in fact the courier. When he eased up the floorboard and opened the satchel, he had his answer. It was full of crisp bank notes in denominations of $10 and $20 bills. His hands now started to tremble as he fanned the notes. It was a small fortune. It had to be a thousand dollars or more. The only honest money he had ever earned in his life was from manual labour at less than two dollars a day. What he now held in his hands had to be worth several years of hard toil. It would not last forever, but it would provide for immediate respite. And then his elation turned to the danger on the streets. Once again, he had to run, somewhere far away and safe, where he could hide and start over again, but this time as a different man. A man with the means to do as he pleased.

WHEN SEAN KELLY arrived in Leadville on April 3, 1888, he was wearing a new suit and sporting a new name—George Kennedy. It was the perfect place to hide amongst the wealth and machinery of mining, silhouetted in the headframes, hoist houses and smelter stacks. But it was the other side of this prosperity that really caught his attention. The one that spawned greed and pleasure.

To keep control of vice, Mayor Horace Tabor had hired an Irishman, Martin Duggan, who had worked as a miner, muleskinner, and enforcer of order in saloons from Colorado Springs to Grand Junction. Duggan had proved his worth over the following ten years, albeit with a dubious approach to the law that made enemies. He also had a taste for the drink and his tenure had been broken through numerous misdemeanours, yet each time he was recalled as no one else could do the job.

The two Irishmen were never to meet, but their paths were to cross. At around four in the morning on April 9, when Kennedy had been in town for less than a week, Duggan was shot in the back of the head by an unknown assailant outside the Texas House. Gossip implied it was a setup. By mid-morning, George Kennedy, along with half a dozen other new arrivals to town, was being questioned as to who he was and where he had been in the earlier hours.

Unprepared and thinking on his feet, Kennedy concocted a story that he was visiting from Ireland and wanted to see a silver boomtown. His new suit and ability to pay his board in advance with a crisp $20 bill, supported his account as a man of means. However, the mayor had a nose for the twisting of the truth and chose to probe further.

On tripping over his new name of George, he was forced to back pedal. "What if I told you, I had a colorful past?" he offered by way of explanation.

"Go on,' said the mayor.

'One I would prefer to keep quiet.'

'That's not an uncommon occurrence here. Does it include being on the wrong side of the law?"

"I would prefer not to answer, but I can assure you, I had nothing to do with the shooting of your marshal."

"I know, your landlady vouched for you."

"So, what do you want with me?"

The mayor leaned back in his chair. "Our marshal was a hands-on man. When a conman tricked several dance hall girls into buying fake jewellery, he hunted the man down, beat him and made him return all the money he had taken. Does that sound like justice to you?" Before Kennedy could answer, the mayor continued, 'Because it does to me."

George Kennedy willingly agreed, "It does."

"If I went looking into your past, would you be in serious trouble?"

Kennedy was silent.

"I'll take that as yes. You look like you can handle yourself. Can you fight? Do you carry a gun?"

"I can fight, and I don't need a gun. I'm Irish, I carry a *shillelagh."*

"That would suit me. Knocking heads together works best in disputes around here. And we can keep it out of the courts."

Kennedy caught on. "Are you offering me a job?"

"I'm offering you protection. Your past is safe with me, and I don't care what your name is or what you have done, but I need another Irishman to be our new marshal."

This most unexpected offer startled Kennedy, but he knew not to look this lucrative gift horse in the mouth. 'When do I start?"

The answer was an emphatic, "Now."

This could have been a new beginning, a chance to put his life back on track. However, when a man who knows only violence and immorality is put in charge of its temptations, is it little wonder that he will indulge. Kennedy was a man who was used to having his way and taking what he wanted, and into his world stumbled Maggie.

IT WAS THE eve of Jacob and Maggie's second wedding anniversary when tragedy struck. The previous years had been demanding and tough. Jacob was on constant call as the intense nature of underground mining took a heavy toll on machinery, requiring replacement parts, grease, and oils. To build up an inventory of parts and lubricants, Jacob had been forced to borrow heavily. Maggie was aware of the debt as she did the bookkeeping, but fortunately, cashflow remained steady and the monthly repayments had been made on time. It was all for the greater good they told each other, they were building a future as a family, and Maggie had just fallen pregnant. Her girlish fantasies had been left behind. She had matured and the fondness for Jacob had turned into true love. She looked forward to their future and being a mother.

When Jacob left that fateful morning, Maggie was grating flakes from a bar of soap. It was Monday—laundry day. He pecked her on the cheek, she smiled, blew away hair that had fallen across her face, and he was gone. She wanted to ask about the church picnic at the lake the following weekend, but it could wait till evening.

The accident occurred less than an hour later up on Carbonate Hill, when a steel hoist cable from the headframe snapped, sending the miners' cage into freefall down a 248-foot vertical shaft. Jacob was the only occupant. When his crushed body was retrieved from the sump and returned to the surface some four hours later, it was covered in blood, dirt, grime, and oil. On receiving the news, Maggie went into immediate shock and miscarried later that evening.

What followed was a cascade of mind-numbing events from the funeral to the notice of foreclosure on the business. Eviction from her home was now pending, so she sought assistance from their bank. They were less than helpful. The situation was desperate when her eye caught the note of condolence from the mayor. It was her last chance. She wrote seeking aid and his return letter advised her to speak directly to Marshal Kennedy who would act as his agent.

WHEN THE NEW marshal saw Maggie in her vulnerable state, he saw opportunity. He proposed that they meet the following evening, across from the opera house at the Board of Trade, which had a discreet entrance at the rear. Maggie felt uneasy, but what choice did she have?

She arrived with trepidation still in mourning dress. His greeting seemed cool but cordial as he ushered her into the dim backroom, closing the door and offering her a seat upon the sofa. On a side table was a small glass of tonic refreshment and not wanting to be impolite she accepted and took a sip. It was sweet with the smell of cloves. He persisted in ensuring that she taste some more.

The banter that followed, as he sat down beside her, was inane but Maggie remained polite and took another sip of the tonic. When he leaned in, she could smell liquor on his breath. She felt uncomfortable and confused, they were alone, he was too close, and she began to feel a little lightheaded.

"I need to go," she heard herself say.

He wasn't listening.

"I need to go, now," she repeated but her voice was being smothered from a pounding in her ears.

"Why? You came for help, let me help you."

She needed to put an end to it. "Not this way."

"There is no other way. That's why you came to me."

"I came to you because I was advised to do so, and you are the law."

"I'm more than the law."

Maggie felt clammy.

"You need a savior and if it isn't me, then who is it?"

The conversation was confronting.

"Relax." Kennedy handed her the glass.

Maggie shook her head, and it began to spin.

Kennedy's hand encircled her wrist firmly. "Let's have a toast," he said, lifting her arm as he tried to place the small green glass in her hand. "I can help you, and you can help me. You were married, so you know what a man requires."

Maggie had trouble comprehending. She'd never heard such words.

"You give, I take, then give back. You need finance, I can arrange that finance. It is a transaction of mutual benefit."

The fabric ruffles of her dress made a slipping sound as he hoisted it up past her calf towards her knee. She stiffened as a hand touched her thigh and began to rub. How could this be happening? She wanted to call out to the muffled voices of men in the room beyond. Yet, as she opened her mouth all she could do was gasp in small breaths. Her mind whirled as if in a dream as a strong hand roughly forced her legs apart, fingers probing. The weight of his body now pressing down. She twisted and squirmed, her arms pushing back as all strength seem to drain away. She felt faint and detached as a tiredness consumed her body and all went dark.

MAGGIE WOKE ALONE with a foggy mind, her dress still hoisted above her knees. Memory was fragmented yet she knew of her violation and felt soiled. She made her way home in the dark and on bolting the door, was overwhelmed with shame. It was to remain for the following days and weeks and felt like a weight upon her shoulders, making her stoop. She kept her gaze downcast, not wanting to make eye contact, in fear the dishonour could be seen upon her face. In the pit of her stomach, she felt nauseous, as if seasick and on the verge of throwing up, and in her head, she blamed herself, arguing and demanding answers to her foolishness for being lured into his trap. At night, remorse consumed her sleepless hours. Her life, once solid as a rock, had been blown apart as if by dynamite. It was all she could think about, and it seemed as if her mind was beginning to unravel. She asked herself if this was how it would be forever, condemned to a life sentence. Dark thoughts began to gather as she desperately searched for a way out of this unbearable misery. Was there only one solution, to end it all and join her beloved Jacob?

Fortunately, it was a fresh dawn of brilliant sunlight that cleared Maggie's head. Why should she surrender and throw away her future. Why should she bear the guilt. Was she not lured by the devil himself to satisfy his lust. Surely, she was due justice. But where could she go. The law was the perpetrator, there was no one else, just her alone. Then, as she quizzed her mind, an unthinkable proposal presented. Was it even possible, she wondered, and did she have the courage and resolve to see it through?

MAGGIE'S EYES WERE set on the gun in her hand. "I just thought I would need a smaller one."

"If you go smaller and lighter, then you will forfeit range and caliber. The Remington .32 pocket revolver is easy to carry and conceal, chambers five shots, and is still powerful enough to protect you from harm."

Maggie looked confused. "Will one shot kill a man?"

"Well, that depends on the range, the size of the man and what he is wearing. It will penetrate to reach the vital organs under most conditions, but one shot, one kill is difficult. That's why you have five shots with this pistol."

"Here," said the gunsmith, "I'll show you how it works." He took the handgun and explained how to load cartridges into each chamber and cock the hammer with her thumb. He then showed her how to squeeze the spur trigger and remove empty cartridges.

Maggie paid acute attention then followed his instruction by loading and unloading empty cartridges several times before saying, "I'll take it."

He placed a box of ammunition on the counter. It was labelled 20 x .32 caliber short rimfire cartridges. "Oh, I won't need that many. Just five, one for each chamber."

"Ma'am, are you a good shot?"

"I don't know yet. I've never fired a pistol before."

The gunsmith placed a second box on top of the first box of ammunition. "This one is on me," he said. "Find yourself some open land, back behind the smelters, away from everybody and place a tin can on a rock five paces away. Take aim and fire. When you hit that tin can, step back five paces and do the same again. Keep doing that all the way back to twenty-five paces, which for you will be about forty feet. Only then will you have a feel for the gun and the confidence to hit a target with your first shot."

"That sounds simple enough."

The gunsmith just said, "In theory, yes."

Maggie returned two days later.

The gunsmith looked up. He was prepared, "You wish to return the pocket revolver?"

"No, I wish to purchase more cartridges."

"Oh. Another box?

'Three."

"So how is the practice going?" He turned his head to hide his smile of amusement.

Maggie lifted her chin in defiance. "Not very well."

"What mark are you up to?"

"Five paces."

"And you are out of ammunition?"

Maggie nodded.

"But you *have* hit the can?"

She slowly shook her head. "Not yet."

As he took the boxes from the shelf, he asked, "Would a little coaching help?"

"If you could provide instruction, that would be most helpful."

"Not me, ma'am. I just sell and maintain guns. You need a shooter, someone who knows how to hold his aim and nerve at the same time."

"And you know such a man?"

The gunsmith looked a little uneasy. "I do, but...."

"But?"

"You're going to have to do it his way." The gunsmith's face pinched as he knew that ex-marshal Charles Webb could be somewhat repetitious in his methods. "He's good, that I can promise. You just need to follow his instruction and without question."

MARSHAL WEBB, I believe you come with good credentials."

"Ma'am, that I don't know, but I can shoot straight when I need to."

"And you are confident that you can teach me to do the same?"

"Nope."

Maggie scowled. "Then why should I pay you for tuition?"

"I can teach you to hit a tin can, but I'm guessing you purchased that gun for other reasons. If you want to protect yourself from an opponent who is trying to kill you, then you need to hold your nerve and shoot straight. I can teach some of that, but in the end, it must come from within."

The ex-marshal pushed the pistol firmly into the web of Maggie's hand and explained how to tighten her grip. "Now pick a point of aim."

Maggie closed her left eye.

"No, keep both eyes open."

"Why?"

"With both eyes open you will still instinctively find your point of aim, while being aware of what is going on around your target when under attack."

"What makes you think I might end up in a situation where I am under attack?"

Webb paused, but only for a moment. "Because you went and got yourself a gun."

"But I may just wish to carry it, just in case, Marshal Webb."

"You don't buy a horse to feed and not ride. And it's Charlie, I lost my badge some time ago."

Next came the explanation on how to lock the elbows and hold the pistol using both hands.

"Keep the pistol high, now lower your head a little and look over the top of the barrel to your point of aim. Then pull back on the hammer."

"But it's not loaded."

"I know." It was said with schoolmaster authority. "Watch to see if the barrel moves off your target."

"It did."

"I want you to keep pulling back and releasing the hammer until the barrel doesn't move."

It was easier said than done and after just ten minutes her arms were heavy, and the barrel was constantly drifting off target.

"Take a rest," came the welcome order.

Maggie was clearly exasperated with both the process and results. "Is this necessary?" she questioned. "I have yet to fire a shot."

"Yes," was the curt reply. "And just think of all the ammunition you're saving."

Practice continued in ten-minute sequences and Maggie realised it was fruitless complaining. The conversation was all one way with short repetitive instructions calling on her to concentrate, inhale, hold, breathe out, keep a firm grip, stop sagging, straighten up.

"Okay," came the call. "We're done for the day."

"But I haven't fired a shot."

"No, that will come tomorrow or maybe the day after."

Maggie was furious. "This is my gun and my ammunition, and I want to shoot."

Charlie reluctantly relented. "Okay, one shot."

"One shot?"

"And on my instructions."

She yielded to the demand, being too tired to muster an argument.

The directions that came were almost soothing as she loaded up, drew in a breath, raised her arms, aimed, pulled back on the hammer, and squeezed the trigger. The crack of the shot was instantaneous, and the tin can flew up into the air. She had done it. She had finally hit her target and the exhilaration removed every ounce of tiredness.

Charlie nodded slowly, "From here on in it's going to be practice, practice, and more practice.

While Maggie was thinking, *practice and planning.*

THE SHOWDOWN CAME on ground of Maggie's choosing. She knew Kennedy's routine in detail and waited just down from the hardware store on Fifth Street, at the junction with Pine. She averted her eyes from the spire of Saint George's Episcopal church, lest her conscience be pricked, then saw him appear on the other side of the street, on his way back to the Board of Trade. He caught sight of Maggie, tall, straight of back, and faltered for a moment before walking on.

"I've come to kill you," she announced in a clear strong voice.

He kept walking, lifting an arm to signal that he had heard her.

"You have nothing to say?"

He looked back over his shoulder dismissively. "I'm busy, make an appointment."

"My appointment is with you. *Now.*"

He stopped, turned his head, and spat, then kept walking.

"And *your* appointment is with the devil." Maggie's pronouncement caused a few who happened to be passing by to pause, as they tried to make sense of this occurrence.

Kennedy finally stopped and turned to see Maggie pointing her small revolver in his direction. "What? He mocked. "You think you are going to shoot me dead from over there with that pea shooter."

The nervousness that she had felt earlier, in anticipation of this confrontation, had gone. She was ready and her hand steady, fixed at the point of aim in the centre of his chest some fifty feet away. In her mind, Charlie was with her, standing back over her shoulder and providing instruction to concentrate, pace her breathing, keep a firm grip and have confidence.

"No," said Maggie with a voice strong and defiant. "It will take more than one shot but that's okay, I have five."

"You'd be lucky hit a barn door."

"Try me."

"Stop being stupid, woman, you—"

Maggie interrupted. "What you did to me deserves punishment."

"You have no proof against me to put before a court of law."

"I have no intention of going to a court of law. If I want justice, I must do it myself."

"Shoot me?" The words came with a smirk. "Because, if that is your intention, you better do it now." The large hulking figure of George Kennedy lifted his *shillelagh* high and lunged forward in attack.

Calmly and without hesitation Maggie squeezed the trigger. The .32 bullet fired and, in an instant, hit the centre of the Kennedy's chest forty feet away.

The second shot penetrated his heavy clothing, entering close to the first wound. Yet Kennedy remained on his feet and kept advancing, letting out a roar, his shillelagh held high.

At twenty feet, her third shot found its mark low in the abdomen just above the belt. He stumbled, but kept upright and continued-on, the shillelagh being swung like a club in battle. Still Maggie held her nerve and her revolver with a firm grip.

It was the fourth shot taken at ten feet that felled Kennedy. It was aimed at his groin, below the previous wound to the stomach. The momentum from the wild charge carried Kelly forward to fall upon his knees at Maggie's feet. The *shillelagh* on the ground behind him.

One shot remained.

Maggie had no thoughts of continued recrimination or malice, it was time to put the pain and remorse behind her, to forgive herself and start over. She was only twenty-two years of age with a lifetime ahead to mend her soul, to make her own way once more, free from threats and intimidation.

Those who had stopped to watch these events seemed to sense what was about to happen and slowly turned their backs and moved away, as if not wanting to bear witness. Maggie kept the barrel aimed directly at Kennedy's face, between the eyes that blazed with vengeance as his mouth continued to spew vile words, and gently squeezed the trigger one more time.

—Leigh Alver is an Australian writer of ten Western novels published under the pen name of Lee Clinton in the Black Horse Western (BHW) series. The UK publishing house responsible for the BHW series has now discontinued that line of books, however, the author's novels remain available in digital form worldwide via Amazon. In the meantime, he has now turned his hand to short stories as he continues with his love of the American Western. Lee lives in one of the most isolated cities in the world, in Western Australia, the largest of the Australian states, which is mostly arid desert but rich in minerals and home to some two million head of beef cattle. He is now retired after a career in the military, which saw service in Vietnam, the US, and UK. His Western titles include, Dark Horse, Devine Wind, No Coward, *and* Reaper.

DROVER IN LOVE

JAMES A. TWEEDIE

"SO, WILL, ARE ya comin' or not?"

"Nah, don't feel up to it."

"What? You don't like the ladies anymore?" Poke laughed.

It was a Saturday night in 1878, and the team of drovers had spent the previous four weeks running two-thousand head of Longhorns near four-hundred miles along the Western Trail from Texas to Dodge City, Kansas.

The cattle had been checked in at the stockyard that morning and Poke and the rest of the boys had bathed and dressed up as best they could under the circumstances.

"Nah, I like the ladies, but I'm thinkin' it's time I settled down with a real woman 'stead o' one of them flowsy-blowsy dancehall girls."

"Them's real women to me," Chet chimed in with an eager grin, "and there's only so many to go'round, so's we'd better scoot on into town or we'll be late fer the roundup!"

"C'mon, Will." Poke added. "What's the point of ridin' all this way and then diggin' yerself a dry well?"

"Nah, you boys go on and git—have yourselves a good time and don't worry yourselves none 'bout me, hear?"

"Your loss," Poke shouted as he and Chet left Will behind in the bunkhouse they were sharing with thirty other men—each as saddle-sore from the trail as they were.

Will Rutherford was 21-years old and tired of eating dust.

Home had been Independence, Missouri, where he'd been too young to soldier his way into the Civil War.

Missouri was a slave state and although it stayed with the Union, there were just about as many for one side as the other. Will's older brother, Andrew, signed on with the Confederacy even though their father had forbidden it. Will never did decide what side he was on, although he was inclined toward Dixie for the sake of his brother.

He was fifteen when the war ended and his brother returned home broken by what he'd seen and done. Andrew's anger spewed out in all directions. There was one day when he might well have shot his Pa if Will hadn't grabbed his brother's cocked and loaded pistol and run out of the house with it.

The arguing and feuding got so bad that Will left home before he turned sixteen. He headed west and worked in a Kansas City stockyard for two years before hiring himself out as a drover.

Now, three years later, he was done with that, too.

He was feeling sulky.

No girl wants to marry a drover, he figured.

He considered homesteading in Nebraska.

Five years improving the land if I'm going to keep it, he thought. I'd be 26-years old and maybe a girl would marry me then... but where would I find a girl in some god-forsaken corner of Nebraska?

He followed that thought with another.

I'd have to go back to Kansas City, or Omaha, or back to Independence to track one down. So why not just move there in the first place? I could find a job, go to church, and find a girl singing in the choir, like Pa found Ma.

Thinking about home made him think that maybe his Pa would take him back and let him work at the mercantile he owned and ran in Blue Springs, a small place where he catered to the needs of farmers and folks traveling to the west.

I know the business, he thought, having helped his Pa at the store since he was a cub.

But the thought of working with his brother turned him off to that idea.

Early the next morning, while his trail partners were sleeping off their hangovers, Will quietly slipped on his best clothes and snuck away. Once in town, he collected his pay, sold his horse and saddle, and headed over to the train station to buy a ticket back to Missouri.

When he got to the station, he had second thoughts.

What the hell am I doing? he asked himself as he sat in the lobby and began sulking again.

A young woman sat down on a bench directly across from him.

Her dress was dark blue and modest. Even so, as was the fashion, it was fitted at the top to show her femininity and flared at the waist to show off the curve of her hips.

Her long dark-brown hair was pulled into a bun on which sat a small straw hat with a feathered plume.

She wore no makeup and, as far as Will was concerned, she looked fine without it.

So beautiful, he sighed to himself as he felt his body stir to life.

When her blue eyes locked onto his own, he realized he had been rude for the staring and was embarrassed by it.

"Yes?" she asked. "Is there something you want to say? You seem to be quite interested in looking at me?"

His face flushed red.

"Yes, ma'am," he stammered. "I mean, no, ma'am... I was just... ah, thinkin' how you look just like my sister, uh.. well, back home in Missouri. And, well... I guess I was feelin' just a little homesick and... I'm sorry for if I was starin'...."

To his surprise, she burst out laughing. Not the demure hand-in-front-of-the-mouth titter he might have expected from such a prim and proper looking young lady, but a full-out laugh that would have been more suited to a saloon than a public place like the lobby of a train station.

"What's so funny?" he asked.

"You don't have a sister, do you?" she smiled.

"I do, too, have... a... sister—" he began, but then thought better of it. He smiled, as his thoughts shifted into a new direction. "Nah, It's a lie, sure enough, but I'd tell it again if I thought I could get away with it."

"Where are you headed?" she asked with a boldness that surprised him. "Back east to see your sister?"

For some reason, her question triggered the memory of a verse from one of the stories his Pa used to read from the Bible every evening before he and Andrew were tucked into bed.

"Wither thou goest, I will go. And your people will be my people, and your God will be my God."

At that moment, Will had no interest in traveling anywhere except wherever it was this woman was going.

He felt as if his future depended on what he said next.

"West. I'm heading west." He was surprised at what he had just said, but he added to the surprise by asking, "And you? Where are you headed?"

"Same as you. West."

"To Denver?" Will asked.

"Beyond," she said. "Leadville."

She paused, perhaps wondering if she had already said more than a single woman traveling alone ought to reveal.

"Me, too," Will replied, not exactly sure where Leadville was. "I mean Denver . . . and maybe farther. I haven't decided yet."

What Will wanted to ask next was, *"Will you marry me? I'd really like to marry you."*

But what he said was, "I'm traveling alone and it would sure be nice if we could keep talking like this while we're on the train. If'n it's all right with you...."

"Yes," she said. "That would be nice. I'd like that."

She paused again before adding, "The town bought me a Second-Class ticket, so if you're in the First-Class car, I guess it won't work out."

"Hell!" Will said, immediately regretting his choice of words. "If'n I were in First Class, I'd-a brung you on as my guest, but seein' that we're both Second Class, I won't have to do it no-ways. Now, if you'll excuse me, I must pay for my ticket."

The ticket to Denver emptied his pockets of more money than he'd planned to spend, but as he looked back across the lobby at his new companion, he took to thinking about it the way a gambler places his bet on the table while hoping for the best.

With ticket in hand he turned around in time to see a well-dressed man with a frock coat and a top hat stride across the lobby. The woman in the blue dress rose to greet him and they drew close enough to plant a kiss on each other's cheek.

Will's heart fell at the sight of it as he realized he'd lost his bet before his hand had been played out.

Now what the hell am I going to do in Denver? he asked himself.

Maybe there's a girl in Colorado who wants to get hitched, he answered himself without much enthusiasm.

HE FELT MORE sulky than ever, and found a place to sit as far from the happy couple as he could.

"Sir?"

The question startled him.

Standing in front of him, hat in hand, was the man who had just kissed the woman he had dreamed of marrying.

"Yes?" Will answered, afraid that he was about to be challenged for some offense he may have caused.

"Adelaide tells me that you have offered to accompany her on the train to Denver," he said. "As her brother, I am bound to be assured of her safety and well-being in the matter. I ask you, sir, to offer me some evidence of your good character."

The comment moved Will forward a few steps, seeing as he now knew the name of the woman and had learned that the man was neither her husband nor her fiancé.

But the request for proof of his good character threw him.

He couldn't call in Poke or Chet to vouch for him and he wasn't carrying what the upper crust might call a "letter of recommendation."

"All I've got is what you're lookin' at," he said as he stood and stared the man straight in the eye. "Your sister is smart, sweet, and funny, and I swear to you that if any man looks at her wrong, or makes unwanted advances, or threatens her in any way, I shall stand in her defense without any thought for my own safety or well-being."

Will had no idea where those words came from, and yet they came out of his mouth sounding like something the man standing in front of him might have said and not at all like the rough-edged talk of a drover.

"I see, sir, that you are a gentleman," the man answered with a slight bow, "and I shall hold you to your word and entrust my sister to your care."

He turned and offered his sister a nod of approval before saying, "And now I must bid you, *adieu.*"

With that, the man placed his hat back on his head and left the station by the way he had entered it.

By calling him a "gentleman," Adelaide's brother had suddenly elevated Will to a social class to which he had never before dared to aspire. And whoever Adelaide was, he now felt bold enough to assume the airs of being her equal.

Slowly, he rose and did his best to sashay across the lobby where he once again sat on the bench opposite the woman with whom he now found himself in love.

For sure as sure, love had taken him hostage to Adelaide as sure as a cow bonds to a newborn calf.

But for all the pretense, his boots gave him away.

"I see you're a horseman," she said, smiling the way a woman does when she knows she is being clever. "For your boots bear the marks of having worn spurs."

Will hesitated, unsure whether to continue the ruse or to come clean with the truth of who he was.

He'd already been caught in one lie and didn't think his chances of accompanying Adelaide to Denver would survive if she caught him in another. So, taking yet another gamble, he said what had to be said.

"These boots are who I am," he confessed. "I'm nothing more than a cowhand—a drover moving herds from Texas to Dodge."

Most folks know there are ways to say something without saying more than necessary, but Will went one step too far when he added, “And usually, I don’t look or smell as good as I do now. In fact, on the trail I sometimes can’t even stand the smell of myself.”

He caught the misstep immediately, but it was too late to take it back. But for the second time the woman surprised him by exploding into a fit of laughter that, if anything, was even louder than the first.

When she stopped laughing, she took a deep breath and began talking. “I believe you just met my brother, Philippe. He fancies himself quite the dandy and has taken up gambling as a profession. He doesn’t look the part now, but he used to be a bare-knuckle boxer who fought for money. ‘Fisticuffs’ is what he liked to call it. His chosen career scandalized our family, just as his gambling does today, but you should know that there were days when he smelled so bad—from his chewing tobacco and the sweat, dung and horse urine he picked up from the street dirt—that it was all I could do to keep my stomach from turning inside out! But look at him now—and look at you—all dressed up for riding the rails instead of riding the trail.”

Will felt like a condemned man who’d just received a full pardon.

“I’ve never met a drover before,” she continued with pleasant frivolity. “In fact, until this trip I’ve never traveled farther west than Ohio. You must entertain me with stories of your adventures while we are on the train.”

If cowboys could be kings, at that moment Will would have been wearing a crown.

For the next thirty-two hours, they sat facing each other as the Great Plains rolled past on both sides of Denver line of the Kansas Pacific Railway Company.

But neither of them paid any mind to the passing scenery, nor did their conversation stall, their story-telling falter, or their banter waver through the long hours of the night.

For each had become enamored with the other and their delight in being together led them to laugh so freely and so often that the train conductor had to tell them to hush for the sake of the other passengers, and that more than once.

Will learned that Adelaide had completed more education than he had ever seen in a woman. She not only could read and write, but she could do it in English, French, Latin and Greek. She had been to London, Paris, and Rome and was excited to have been hired as the new schoolteacher for the growing silver mining boom town of Leadville, Colorado—a hundred miles west of Denver and 10,000 feet in the air.

For her part, Adelaide learned the difference between a lariat and a lasso. She learned about cattle trails and how the different tribes charged different fees for each steer that crossed their particular part of the Oklahoma Territory. She learned how to tell the difference between a Kiowa, Comanche, Cherokee, Shawnee, and Apache and how to stop a stampeding herd of Longhorns.

Shortly before they arrived in Denver, Will confessed his love for Adelaide and asked for her hand in marriage.

To his surprise, instead of laughing, she asked if he would accompany her to Leadville.

"Then ask me again in six months." She smiled. "Until then, we can be friends."

As things played out, Will proved to be a better gambler than Philippe. For he bet all that he had, and when it came to winning the love of Adelaide, he ran the table.

—James A. Tweedie has lived in California, Utah, Scotland, Australia, Ha-

waii, and presently next to a Pacific Ocean beach in southwest Washington. He has published six novels, three collections of poetry, and one collection of short stories with Dunecrest Press. His western stories and poetry have appeared in both print and online media. He claims to be an optimist.

NOT IN LEADVILLE

JD ARNOLD

FOUNDED IN 1877, Leadville, Colorado, was a boomtown. By 1880, the new town had twenty-eight miles of streets, many of which were gaslit, a municipal water system, five churches, three hospitals, six banks, and a school for 1,100 students. Many of its buildings were constructed of bricks. The post office was the busiest between St. Louis and San Francisco. The Tabor Opera House was doing a robust business as was the Windsor Hotel. The town's population was over 15,000, exceeded in Colorado only by Denver. The root cause of the boom was silver!

The rush of miners swelled in 1874 when silver was discovered in the black sand waste product of the placer gold mining operations near Leadville at California Gulch, circa 1860 to 1873. By 1876 several lead-silver lode deposits had been discovered and the money flowed like quicksilver on glass. Fortunes were made and lost, but for the most part, all the folks generally did well, as long as the silver production continued. Things were coming up roses. However, all was not bliss for some residents.

IN THE DIMINISHING light of a gray day in the early autumn of 1879, three brothers huddled together in a small canvas tent that just barely kept them dry. The rain was light but steady, and thankfully there was no wind. Underneath the open tent flap, they had a small bed of charcoal burning in a cast iron skillet with a small metal grate over the coals. On the grate, sat a tin pot full of water. A young man attended it under the curious eye of a teen-aged boy. The other, young man, sat cross-legged at the opposite end of the tent. He stared out at the muddy street and puddles of rainwater here and there. There was no talking among them. The teenager sat in between them, hugging his knees to his chest. There was little space between any of them as they were packed into the small tent cheek by jowl.

"Why is the water taking so long to boil?" the boy asked in his native tongue.

"We are up very high in the mountains. Water is always slow to boil in mountains. There it goes now. Hand me the rice bag."

The man poured two cups of rice into the boiling water. He let it return to boil, removed it from the heat, covered it and set it aside. From a canteen he poured more water into another pot and placed it on the grate. And, still into another pot, he shaved thin slices of dried pork belly from a slab he pulled from his pack and placed that on the grate to cook. As it heated, it filled the little tent with aromatic steam. The water in the other pot boiled and he poured in black tea leaves and let them steep. When all was ready, he used a spoon to scoop the rice and pork belly into small lacquered bowls, stuck chopsticks into the rice mixture and handed the bowls to the other man and boy followed by small cups of hot tea.

Lastly, he served himself.

While the men and boy consumed their meal, the younger one said, "Do you think we will work tomorrow if it is still raining?"

Although not much older, the other one said, "No. You cannot dig a ditch in the mud. The rain has to stop pretty soon today, or they will not let us dig tomorrow."

"How much did you say they were paying?"

"One dollar, fifty cents a day."

"Not much more than the railroad did."

"Yeah."

"I am thinking of returning to Qingyan. Not making any big fortune here like we thought we would."

"Well, remember we heard it was a boomtown. Wonder why they call it Leadville?"

"I do not know. I just know I need to save enough money to get back to Qingyan. Bringing our little brother here was a big mistake. I wish our parents had not sent him."

"I am pulling my weight," the boy said. "You cannot complain about me."

"You know Confucious says to respect our elders," the older young man reminded him.

"I respect and obey them. But I do not have to agree with them."

"Yes, Chih-Cheng, you are pulling your weight, but I am still responsible to the family for you."

"I can take care of myself, Chih-Ming. You don't have to worry about me."

"Humpf. What do you think, Chun-Chieh?"

"Well, I am young still. Just twenty years old. So, I don't think much about anything beside myself. And now I want to return home." He smiled half-heartedly.

"All right. Look. The rain has stopped. Want some more tea?"

"Well, I am a few years younger than you and I miss our Jui life." He grasped some rice and pork with his chopsticks and deposited them in his mouth. Some tea, more pork and rice, more tea and soon the hunger pains were gone.

By the time they had finished their supper and rinsed clean their food preparation and eating vessels in the creek behind them, the clouds began to break up and a big full moon shone through brilliantly. "Why are you so mopey?" Chih-Ming asked of Chun-Chieh.

"Do you not see the full moon? It is the time of the Moon Festival. In Guiyang the Jiaxiu Tower will be bright with hanging lanterns and the people will all be celebrating and dancing. They will be eating moon cakes. And here we are wasting away in Leadville, eating slop."

"We are not wasting. We have work. That is something."

"Yes. But they won't let us work in the mines and won't let us make claims on creeks to sluice for gold. No fortune for us. That is why we are wasting. I think I am going to write home for permission to return."

"You think you should do that? You know there is still war in the province."

"I think so. More tea, please."

IN THE MORNING, the wind was up. It came out of the south and there was a fall chill in the air. It carried on it the thick black smoke of the smelters, foundries, iron works and machine shops closest to town. The smoke obscured the new light of the morning, but nobody noticed.

The brothers stood waiting with thirteen of their countrymen in the muddy street, off to the side, at the hitching rail of the back entrance to the new courthouse on Harrison Avenue. They all had all they possessed on their backs—tents, blankets, sparse clothing, kitchen and eating utensils. The clothes they wore were threadbare with mismatched patches sewn on here and there. Their shoes were worn thin, and their hats were rumpled and out of shape. Presently, a man dressed in tan khaki pants and a tan khaki coat emerged from the door and stepped out onto the porch. "Too wet today, boys. Come back tomorrow. We'll try again," he said and then did an about-face to disappear through the door he came from. The sixteen men slowly and quietly went their separate ways.

The three brothers separated from the other men and squatted in an alley. "What will we do now?" Chun-Chieh directed his question to Chih-Ming. "We cannot afford to lose a day of work."

"Let's go to the rail yard. They always have some kind of work," Chih-Cheng said with his youthful enthusiasm showing in his eager smile and shining black eyes.

"Yes, let's do that," Chin-Ming said. They stood and quietly padded through the alleys in a northerly direction, that generally paralleled Harrison, until they came out into the open field behind the depot. They ran across the field, crossed the tracks, and stopped behind the huge coal crib where they took time to catch their breath. Chin-Ming led the way to the roundhouse office where a man stood outside and seemed to be directing things. He wore pinstriped engineer bib overalls with a matching hat.

Chin-Ming padded up to him, bowed his head with his hands folded in front and said, "Excuse, sir. We look for work. You have?"

The man frowned at him and gave them all a once-over. "Wal, you can empty the toilet tanks on the coaches. Pays a nickel per coach. And I need to fill in the old and get a new cesspool pit dug. Pay you a dollar for that. You want the job?"

Chin-Ming bobbed his head up and down. "Yes, sir. We want."

"All right. Wait here a minute. I'll be right back to show you what to do."

Chin-Ming bowed his head and backed up two steps. When the man was out of earshot, he said to his brothers in their native language, "He will pay us five cents per coach to empty the toilet tanks. And then a dollar to dig a new pit."

"How many coaches?" Chun-Chieh asked.

"How many did you count when we were coming up here?" Chih-Ming asked of Chih-Cheng.

"Twenty," he said.

"So that is another dollar. We'll make two dollars today. That's better than nothing."

"Yeah. Okay. Here he comes."

"Grab that kettle right there. Yeah. That one. Made it myself from the bottom half of a whiskey barrel. Bring it along. We'll go over to that coach there." They trudged along behind him in the mud. "There. See that yellow valve right there?" He pointed to a valve, painted yellow, protruding from the undercarriage of the coach. "Put the kettle under the valve like this," he said as he slid the kettle under the valve. "Okay. Then you open the valve. Go ahead. You do it."

Chih-Ming looked at him suspiciously as he seemed to have a mischievous gleam in his eyes.

"Go on. Open it."

"You show me."

The man turned dark and growled, "You want the job, you open it."

Chih-Ming stepped up and opened the valve just a little so that a trickle of raw sewage appeared. It stunk and he screwed up his nose.

"Open it all the way."

Slowly Chih-Ming turned the handle so the valve opened fully and the black, stinky slop poured out into the kettle without a drop spilling onto him, contrary to what he suspected the man was attempting to trick him into.

"Okay. There's another valve at the other end of the coach. You do the same thing and then dump the crap into the pit over there. Come on. I'll show you." They arrived at the pit that had a big wooden cover over it. "Lift that cover off."

The muck was bubbling and stinking to high heaven. A horde of flies buzzed around the pit, diving down and flying back up, all in crazy zig-zags and circles. Chun-Chieh and Chih-Cheng set the kettle on the ground and pulled their bandanas up to cover their noses and mouths. Chin-Ming and the railroad man did the same. He motioned for them to pour the slop into the pit, and they did. "Now, when the top gets to right here, you stop and fill it in with this pile of dirt. Dig another pit over here down to your shoulders. I'll bring the shovels directly. Got it?"

Ching-Minh bobbed his head yes.

"Okay. Should be about twenty coaches today. All right. Get to work on all those coaches over there."

The three brothers emptied all the coaches and had the new pit dug by noon. Now they had to wait for the afternoon trains to arrive. Meanwhile, they munched on dried pork belly and by the end of the day when the last train arrived at sunset they were done and collected their wages.

EARLY THE NEXT morning, they collected picks and shovels at the county engineer's yard and marched up East 10th Street, passed the outskirts of town to the hillside just below the road where they were to dig a diversion ditch across the face of the hillside. The ditch was planned to divert runoff from the hillside to the gulch way outside of town.

The sixteen men had been digging steadily for about two hours when a group of six men showed up. Chin-Ming looked up at one of them who wore a shiny tin star on his coat lapel and a pistol in a holster on his hip. He was talking loudly to the county engineer. The two of them stood near the edge of the ditch and the other five were off to the side. He moved closer down the line of diggers so he could hear what they were saying.

"Jacobs, you know the mayor and city council voted on this and approved it," the lawman said. "You know they can't be here. Where'd they come from?"

"Got no idea. But it's county land. Not city."

"Don't give me no trouble or I'll have you up before the JP."

Chin-Ming spoke up and said, "What we do wrong? We just want work. Not bother anybody. This America."

The marshal glared at Chin-Ming and growled, "Yeah, well, you ain't American. Ain't no John Chinaman allowed in Leadville. I don't care what this yahoo says. You got until sundown to clear out a town or we'll beat you to a pulp and drag you out. You understand?"

Chin-Ming let a slight smile come across his lips, bowed his head and said, "Understand."

With a threatening stare, the marshal said to the engineer, "And don't you be bringing any more o' these slant-eyed, yellow varmints back into town or you're liable to end up behind bars. Leadville is too fine a town to put up with this yellow peril." He held his stare for a few seconds, spun on his heel and stomped away. The other four men fell in behind him.

"Mista Jacobs," Chin-Ming said. "We keep working. We get paid for all day?"

"Yes. Just keep going. Get as much done as you can, and I'll pay you for a full day. But you'll have to quit about an hour before sundown so you can get out of town and Marshal Kelly doesn't catch you."

AS THE ORANGE globe grew large and descended rapidly to touch the slope of Mount Massive to the west of town, the three brothers trudged northeast on the road out of town. Under the burden of their heavy packs, they walked with a curve to their backs and a bend of their legs at the knee. Chin-Ming turned his head to look back for the fiftieth time to make sure they weren't followed. And for the fiftieth time he saw the marshal and his deputies sitting their horses on the road at the edge of town, watching the brothers. His eye naturally went to the white church spire, rising high above the town roofs in the center of town behind them. It was most prominent against the backdrop of the green foothills of the Sawatch Range. He sighed and smiled.

"Where are we going now?" Chih-Cheng asked in a slightly croaky voice.

"Yeah. What do we do now?" Chun-Chieh piped up.

"We are going to Blackhawk. Chin Lin Sou is there. He is very important. He manages workers and can get us jobs. Our family knows his family."

"Why didn't we go see him months ago?"

"I don't know. Do you think I know everything? He will get us jobs and you can go home when you have enough money."

"Will you come, too?"

"I don't know."

—Back in the day, when Jeff was a kid, he watched plenty of westerns on TV, read a few books, and always wanted to be a rancher. As it turned out, he never got there. Instead, he is a veteran combat Army aviator, former deputy sheriff, death investigator, and longtime CPA. Now he sort of lives a rancher's life vicariously through the stories he writes.

RATTLERS

BRUCE HARTMAN

ONE-EYED ARLEN ran his cattle on the bottomland along the Arkansas south of Twin Lakes. The men in his outfit were convict labor contracted out of Cañon City, murderers and horse thieves who would have been hung if Arlen hadn't paid hard cash for them. When he heard about the fugitives fleeing south from Leadville—an aging cowpuncher, a Cheyenne woman, and an idiot boy with a hairlip—he sensed another profit opportunity. How could a pitiful group like that stand up against his crew of hardened criminals? And when he heard about the bounty on their heads—$2,000 dead or alive, more than his whole ramshackle herd would fetch—he thought he'd died and gone to heaven.

He intended to keep the bounty for himself. But there was one cowboy, named Clyde—the youngest in the outfit, just eighteen, though said to be a cold-blooded killer—who said the cowhands ought to share it. The boy's face was pale and his eyes as gray as a hawk's. He had thin bloodless lips and he wore a red bandana wrapped tight around his neck. "It wouldn't be right for you to keep that bounty," he told Arlen, "if we're the ones that earn it."

Arlen exploded like fireworks on the Fourth of July. He grabbed a bullwhip off his belt and lashed out at the boy, carving a gash in his cheek as big as his thumb. The boy didn't flinch. He set his cold gray eyes on Arlen, who suddenly looked more scared than angry.

"I don't need no moralizing from the likes of you," Arlen said, flicking the whip in front of him like a rattler's tongue. "If you scumsuckers get any part of that bounty, it'll be out of the kindness of my heart. You hear that? The kindness of my heart."

AN OLD PROSPECTOR named Mose, who'd been driven off his claim years before, lived like a hermit in an abandoned mine above the river, begging food from miners and cattle outfits. Seventy years old, with a wild head of hair and a white beard that straggled down in two halves like a swallow's tail, he drifted down to Arlen's cow camp hoping that one of the hands would share a crust of hardtack and a sip of whiskey. He hated Arlen from long acquaintance, and when he heard the men talk about catching the fugitives he vowed to find them and help them escape. He knew the terrain better than any man in that valley.

The next day the sun blazed brutally hot. Mose, traveling on foot, found the fugitives after sunset as they set up camp in a draw east of the river. His welcome was a shotgun pointed at his heart by an Indian woman with eyes like an obsidian knife.

"Pleased to meet you, too," he said, showing his hands.

A sun-blistered white man appeared behind the woman. "What do you want here?"

"There's men coming you don't want to know. I'm here to help you."

Behind the man he spied a boy of about fourteen crouching low around a pile of wood trying to build a fire. The boy's hair was dark and thick and his mouth was twisted into an idiotic grin. Four horses browsed in the brush behind the boy.

"I say we just shoot him," the woman said, her eyes narrowing.

"It ain't me you need to be afraid of."

The man—his name was Jonathan Hawkins—took a long look at Mose. He was dressed in a crazy quilt of threadbare vests and leggings and a fancy shirt that might have been fifty years old, with no boots. His feet wrapped in cloth tied around with rawhide cord. His eyes were black and deep, like holes bored in a cliff.

He sure didn't look like a bounty hunter.

"I know there's a bounty on your head," the old man said, "but I don't know what you did to earn it. Don't care, neither."

Jonathan stepped beside the woman, who held the shotgun steady, her finger on the trigger. He knew she wouldn't hesitate to blast the old man to kingdom come if he gave her the word. She was a loving and loyal woman, but no sentimentalist. She would do anything to save him and the boy, even though the boy wasn't hers. But for some reason he trusted this old man who claimed he wanted to help them. "It ain't what it seems. We didn't do nothing wrong."

"Then why're you running?"

"Leadville don't like my wife and it don't like me. So the sheriff thought he'd hang a noose around my neck."

"Why so high a bounty, though? Two thousand dollars. You must've killed somebody."

"Somebody killed Clint Bishop. It wasn't me and they know it."

The old man beamed with a kind of joyful astonishment. He lurched toward Jonathan as if he wanted to shake his hand. The woman swung the shotgun toward him and would have pulled the trigger if Jonathan hadn't raised his hand.

"Son, if you killed Clint Bishop, you have my vote."

"No, I didn't, I—"

"I'll shake your hand just for being accused of it."

The woman stepped forward and pushed the shotgun barrels against his chest.

"No, Rachel," Jonathan said. "Don't shoot him."

"He better have a good story to tell," she said.

"Clint Bishop is the snake that hornswoggled me out of my claim. I would've killed him myself if I got the chance."

Jonathan eased the shotgun away from the old man's chest, and with his eyes told the woman to back off. The boy had the fire blazing now and he'd set a pan of water on to boil. "We were about to make some coffee," Jonathan said. "Can we offer you some?"

The old man touched his hat brim. "Name's Mose."

"Jonathan Hawkins. You've met Rachel."

"Indeed I have." Mose arranged his broken teeth into a smile and she glared back at him like a wildcat ready to pounce. "And your boy?"

"Come on, Jesse. Mind your manners."

The boy sidled forward, keeping his eyes down. His twisted grin was permanent, the result of botched surgery on a hare lip. He bowed politely but didn't speak.

"What I wanted to tell you is," the old man said, "your trail ain't hard to follow. Arlen's outfit won't be long in coming."

Arlen? Jonathan didn't know anybody by that name.

"Them boys'll be on you like wolves on a spring lamb. Contract labor from the penitentiary, just waiting to be hung. They don't care who they kill."

Jonathan put on a brave face but he was close to despair. He'd spent most of his life on cattle trails and the shabby towns along them. He knew horses and cattle better than he knew himself or the guile of men. Rachel was a Cheyenne he'd rescued from the army after the battle of

Punished Woman's Fork and again from a deranged, drunken husband ten years later. She'd seen enough hardship and tragedy for three lifetimes. Why on earth had he brought her and his son to Leadville, a city founded on greed and nurtured on crime, a landscape of sinkholes and sulphur fuming from a hundred smelters? It was the closest thing to hell he could have imagined, if not the place itself. They called him a squaw man and played him for a fool, and now he was worth more money dead than he'd ever hoped to see in his lifetime.

"How can you help us?" he asked Mose.

"I know these parts like nobody else. If there's a blade of grass I ain't seen before, it must have just sprouted."

"You can't trust him," Rachel said.

"I'm unarmed, ma'am."

"How do we know you're not luring us someplace where you can turn us in?"

"How do I know Jonathan ain't really a murderer?"

"You have my word on that," Jonathan said.

"A murderer's word, if you are one."

"I ain't a murderer."

"Then tell your lady to put the shotgun down."

Jonathan took Rachel aside and whispered in her ear. She wore a full calico dress like the ones white women wore, but her hair was pulled back in braids. She had been pretty once. Jonathan must have convinced her to back off, at least for the time being. She squatted beside the fire in a heap, the shotgun within easy reach.

"It ain't for nothing they call me Mose," the old man told Jonathan. "I know a place, a day's ride south of here, where you can disappear like the morning mist. It'll be like crossing the Red Sea. You'll make it across but Pharaoh's army won't. Once you're past there you're in the Sangre de Cristos and even the devil won't be able to find you."

ARLEN'S OUTFIT SPENT most of the day preparing to hunt the fugitives. They fed and watered their horses, packed their gear and provisions, and herded their cattle into a steep draw blocked with a rope corral. The men were sulky and quarrelsome, scorning the idea of sharing the bounty out of the kindness of Arlen's heart. Arlen kept their spirits alive by tempting them with the fun they'd have when they caught up with the fugitives. "I don't want you boys to think you get nothing out of this," he told them. "Tonight that squaw will be all yours, to do with as you please."

The men cheered at that, except for Clyde, the pale cowboy whose face Arlen had whipped when he demanded a share of the bounty. Clyde looked paler and more menacing than ever, the wound on his cheek dripping blood and pus that stained the bandana he wore around his neck. The other men hated and distrusted Clyde. He was a born killer and that was all he'd ever wanted to be. Three days shy of his eighteenth birthday, he'd skinned a man alive in Durango and nailed the skin to the courthouse door. The penitentiary stuck him in contract labor to get some work out of him before he was hung. Not everybody believed that story—he was so pale, he looked like he was already dead. Some said they hung him before leasing him out and he wore the bandana to hide the rope burns on his neck.

By sunset, all preparations completed, Arlen's outfit rode out after the fugitives and soon found their trail. In the distance, near the edge of the sky, a coyote howled.

MOSE STOOD SNIFFING the wind as the sky darkened, studying the clouds as they gathered behind the divide. To the east a waning sliver of moon peeked over the mountains. Tomorrow would bring more heat, night-time clouds, possibly a thunderstorm. "We need to skedaddle," he told Jonathan. "Arlen and his crew'll be on their way by now."

"We can't sleep here?"

"You got about two hours. Lucky you brought four horses."

They rode all night, long after the waning moon had fled the sky. Mose knew the terrain even in the darkness. Sand hills, gullies, sudden rocky outcrops gnarled by ancient centuries of water and wind. A wire fence thrown up by some hapless homesteader and abandoned when the creek dried up. A family graveyard, a burnt-out cabin, the rusted ribcage of a covered wagon. Two hours after dawn, when the sun was high enough to sting their sleepless eyes, he led them across a flat of rippled sand to a spring-fed thicket of cottonwoods and cedars where they ate breakfast and watered the horses.

Breakfast was coffee and hard tack and slivers of beef jerky, doled out by Jonathan in equal portions. They ate in silence. The boy kept his eyes down as he stuffed his twisted mouth. Rachel sat across from Mose with the shotgun on her lap.

"Rachel is still itching to shoot you," Jonathan told Mose.

"I can see that."

"I hope she doesn't, but I can't guarantee it."

"Fair enough. Ain't no guarantees in this life."

When breakfast was done they rounded up the horses, which they'd left grazing by the spring, and rode south under a sweltering sky. "Looks like another scorcher," Mose said with an air of satisfaction. "Hot as Hades where we're going."

"Is that a good thing?"

"You'll see."

Jonathan shot a wary glance at Rachel, who rode with the shotgun across her saddle. As they lay together under the darkness, she had confided her suspicions about Mose. On the route he'd led them on, there was no shortage of creeks, exposed rock, and stretches of dry shortgrass where a horse, even four horses, could pass without leaving a trail, but Mose had taken no such precautions. Either he was in league with the bounty hunters, she whispered, or he was one himself, if not a devil intent on leading them to destruction. "Hush," Jonathan said. "Without him we'd be lost."

They rode into the afternoon under the relentless sun. The land was hotter, drier, beckoning with mirages of shimmering ponds and distant watchtowers. Just before sunset they followed the valley into a high desert basin. Dust devils whirled behind them as if to show the way to their pursuers. "How do you know we're not leaving a trail for them bounty hunters to follow?" Jonathan asked the old man.

"I'm sure we are," the old man chuckled. "In fact, I'm counting on it."

ARLEN'S OUTFIT STOPPED at sunset to rest their horses, half dressed, thirsty, wilting under the sun. They dismounted and stood clustered together with their eyes down, hats twirling in their hands. Clyde prowled behind them like a caged animal, his gray eyes restless, the welt on his cheek blistered and throbbing. They'd ridden all night and all day and they knew one thing—in that parched country no kindness would stir in Arlen's heart. And what good would the bounty do them anyway, when they were sent back to Cañon City? A few men joked about the woman, but the others turned away in disgust. What they would do to her wouldn't make the world worth living in.

RIDING AHEAD OF the others, Mose brought his horse to a sudden stop by a shallow creek at the foot of a rocky escarpment. He peered up the slope and at the circle of distant mountains fading into the dusk, sniffing the air like a wolf on the scent of its prey. "This is where we stop."

"Why are we stopping?" Jonathan asked.

"Arlen and his men'll be here in a couple of hours."

"Then shouldn't we keep going?"

"They're coming to kill you and drag your carcass in for the reward. Your lady—what's left of her, that is—they won't even stick under a rock. The idea is to kill them first."

"I ain't a killer."

Mose laughed. "You won't need to do any killing. The Lord made rattlesnakes for a reason." He built a fire near a big fallen cottonwood near the creek and told Jonathan to unpack the food. "You folks better rest a little and have something to eat."

They boiled water for coffee and cooked bacon and eggs in a frying pan. Jesse sat on the cottonwood watching the sparks rise in the wind. Rachel squatted beside him with the shotgun on her lap, facing away from Mose at such an angle that she could watch him, and possibly shoot him, without falling under his gaze.

She didn't trust his eyes.

THE NIGHT WAS moonless and black, trembling with distant thunder. With startling suddenness, invisible clouds wrapped it in a spectral whiteness that lingered for a heartbeat and disappeared.

"Heat lightning," Mose said, as if he'd been waiting for the flash. He lopped a branch off the fallen cottonwood and fashioned a torch about three feet long, dipping one end in the bacon grease to make it catch fire. "Come on," he said, raising the torch. "I want to show you something."

Jonathan and Rachel started to follow, leaving Jesse to tend the fire. "Bring the boy," Mose said. "I know he can hear and I know he ain't a idiot."

He held the torch high as he led them a hundred yards south along the creek. Wading across, they climbed a path up the escarpment to a wide bench of land where calcium deposits had hardened the sand into cement, white and slick and brittle as a whitewashed tomb. An eager wind hissed over the plain.

"On a summer day like this one," Mose said, lowering his torch before the others looked over the rim, "that cement gets as hot as a stove lid. Even at night it stays warm to the touch."

"Can you feel it?" he asked Jesse.

Jesse felt the heat radiating toward his face. He bent down toward the cement and raised his foot over the rim to see if it would warm his boot. The landscape quivered with a low whirring sound that came not from bird or insect or any other creature of the air.

Mose grabbed his elbow and pulled him back. "Wait. You don't want to step there. Wait for the next lightning flash."

Mose stared into the darkness as if he could see the lightning coming. He sucked in a breath and the earth and sky ignited in a silent explosion of white light that lasted two or three seconds, long enough for the four of them to see what had gathered on that godless plain. Hundreds of rattlesnakes stretched and slithered before them, basking in the leftover heat of the day, some coiled, some elongated, some swallowing others and vomiting them out.

"That's what it's like for you folks," Mose said. "Serpents slithering all over the earth, hunting you down."

Jonathan felt his hackles rise. "Why did you bring us here?"

"There's a kid named Clyde rides with Arlen. He ain't human, he's a demon out of hell. You wait and see."

Rachel felt sick to her stomach. She buckled over and retched as if she were trying to expel a rattlesnake. The sound of her coughing and retching was lost in the chorus of whirring and hissing which she had taken for the wind.

MOSE LED THEM back to the camp and carved three more torches from the fallen cottonwood and handed them out. Then he lay down with his ear to the ground, moaning softly. "I hear them about five miles away."

Jesse watered the horses while Jonathan and Rachel gathered the food and gear and packed the saddlebags. Silent lightning flashed in the sky and the plains wavered in and out, pale as solitude, black as forgetting.

"We're getting out of here," Jonathan said.

"Not yet," Mose said, still listening. "Keep the fire alive."

Jesse saddled the horses and sat on the cottonwood staring at the fire, rocking back and forth, kicking his feet. The flames mimicked the snakes' tongues and the green wood hissed and Rachel felt sick again, terrified because she recognized Mose as a devil and Jonathan would not explain why they had placed their trust in him. She pleaded with him to leave without Mose but he told her to wait.

After fifteen minutes Mose, still with his ear to the ground, said, "Two miles. It's time to go."

They dipped their torches in the bacon grease and lighted them in the fire and dowsed it. Then they wrapped blinders on the horses and led them south along the creek, not bothering to cover their tracks. They followed the path up the escarpment and at the rimline they stared into the darkness over the throbbing plain. The hissing and whirring had subsided into the wind. A foul smell hung in the air.

"How are we going to get across this snake pit?" Jonathan asked.

"Just follow me and do what I do."

Mose stepped over the rim twirling his torch and the snakes slithered away rattling and hissing in anger. Jonathan and Rachel followed with the blinkered horses, flailing away any lingering snakes with their torches. The hissing and rattling rose to a roar as the rattlers vowed revenge. By the time Jesse passed, the last snakes were disappearing into cracks and crevices beyond the range of his torch.

"They'll come back out soon enough," Mose chuckled. "Them rattlers can't resist a warm rock."

WHEN THE COWBOYS came—riding just ahead of Arlen—the fugitives huddled on the other side, peering back at them over the writhing plain. They heard the men jangling their reins and calling out to each other as they gathered at the rim before plunging into the unknown. At first the catastrophe announced itself only as sound—heavy tramping and clattering of hooves, then staggering, rearing and screaming, the horses tottering and falling and the cowboys tumbling on and under them crying out in fury and agony as the snakes exacted their revenge against the race of men. Arlen's voice rang out the loudest, cursing his men as much as the rattlesnakes as he tried to register the disaster through his single eye. Then while the men struggled to pull their attackers' fangs out of their throats and faces, lightning flashed—just long enough to show them the landscape of their suffering, fixing that hideous moment forever in time and memory as if it had been captured by some satanic photographer for the annals of hell.

Such a photograph—had it existed at the time—might have been taken by Clyde, the pale cowboy, who stood on the rim overlooking the pitiless plain. He watched the men writhe and flail with no apparent emotion and made no effort to help them, though he had his pistol drawn. But lest it be said that he was hard of heart, it should be recorded that when Arlen crawled to the rim trailing a dozen snakes whose fangs were sunk deep in his throat and his limbs and his one good eye, Clyde, without hesitation, put him out of his misery.

But if Clyde fancied that he would be the one to claim the bounty, he was to be sorely disappointed. By the time he had disposed of Arlen and found his way around the seething plain, the three fugitives, guided by Mose, had slipped into the darkness, leaving no trail behind them, and were well on their way to the Sangre de Cristos, where even the devil wouldn't be able to find them.

—Bruce Hartman has been writing fiction for over fifty years. His current project is a trilogy of novels set in Colorado, Montana, and Oklahoma, focusing on the great cattle boom of the 1870s and 1880s, its catastrophic collapse in the Big Die-Up of 1886-87, and the impact of those events on the men and women who built their lives around the cattle business, as well as on the native people in the region. Bruce traces his roots to the West and lived for many years in Colorado. Currently he divides his time between Colorado and Pennsylvania.

Buffalo Signal by W. Herbert Dunton

THE MOUNTAIN ROSE

BEN HENRY BAILEY

MATTIE GREYSON STIRRED awake as the conductor came down the aisle, ringing a bell loudly.

"Ten minutes to Leadville." Through sleep hazed eyes, she watched him walk through the door, to the next car. Slowly coming to the realization of where she was, she settled back into her seat and looked across at her father, who was reading his Bible.

"I must have dozed off," she said, stretching her stiff muscles.

Morton Greyson just acknowledged with a grunt, his eyes never leaving the holy scriptures. The Denver and Rio Grande train ride had been steady, but the conversation was lacking with her father. The great minister Morton Greyson could throw fire and brimstone from the pulpit and make any sinner repent and give their lives to Jesus. When it came to interactions with his own daughter however, he seemed to keep his distance and only voice judgments when he did speak. The upbringing she had had with her sister Holly was strict, Bible-based and in most aspects lack of fatherly warmth. Mattie figured that had gone away when her mother died years ago.

Opening her bag, Mattie pulled out the letter they had received back in Kansas. Reading it for the hundredth time did not lessen the emotions that she felt the day it arrived. Her eyes only saw the words from the letter that had devastated her world.

We regret to inform you that your kin, Holly Greyson has passed away in Leadville, Colorado.

Those words had brought her and her father by train out from the plains of Kansas to the mountains of Colorado. She took a small leave from the school she taught at and her father begrudgingly left his congregation. They stopped off in Denver and boarded another train, bound for Leadville. The letter had not informed them how her sister had died but they were holding off on any funeral proceedings until there was word from the family.

Morton Greyson had shown little emotion upon reading the letter but simply stated they should go retrieve Holly to bring her home to be buried next to her mother. Holly had never gotten along with her father after their mother had died and their arguments used to wake up the neighbors. Mattie figured this to be partly the reason why her father had run Holly out of the house five years back.

The train pulled into the station as the brakes screeched the iron horse to a stop. Finally closing his Bible, Morton rose to his feet and made his way down the car to the exit door, Mattie a close step behind. When her father had somewhere to go, he would not spend time looking for you to keep up.

Even now at twenty-seven years old, Mattie felt as if she was still the same five-year-old chasing after her father. The station had a couple people standing on the walk but mostly it was empty. A skinny man in a black suit and top hat made his way over to Mattie and Morton.

"Reverend Morton Greyson, I presume?"

"I would be him." Morton replied, eying the stranger intently.

"I am Doctor Todlen. I am the one who sent you the letter about your daughter."

Both men shook hands and Doctor Todlen looked at Mattie and tipped his hat. "Ma'am."

"I appreciate you taking the long journey to our little mining town. I am very sorry for your loss."

The doctor was very thin and had tiny spectacles on the end of his nose. He looked to be in his late forties but maybe not in the best health as skinny as he was. Mattie nodded at the doctor and said "We appreciate you reaching out to us about Holly. Can we see her?"

The man nodded as he adjusted the spectacles. "This way, please."

TODLEN HAD A buggy waiting for them and the drive to the undertaker's office was only five minutes. Mattie was amazed by the mining town she had heard so much about from her sister's letters. Holly had described Leadville as being beautiful and the scenery around the town certainly did not disappoint. The buildings and board walks were crowded and being this high in the mountains, Mattie was a little surprised to see so many people walking down the street. This truly seemed to be a metropolis of the mountains.

Arriving at the undertaker's, Todlen stepped down out of the buggy and offered his hand to Mattie. She felt the anxiety of finally being able to see her sister hit her like a ton of bricks as she stepped down. Standing on the boardwalk, she looked up at the sky and quietly asked God for strength. Her sister died only a week ago, so the shock was still very fresh. Finally bring able to see Holly was almost overwhelming.

The doctor opened the door and Morton stepped in, not allowing Mattie to go first. Laid out in the backroom in a wooden coffin was Holly. The face that had held such joy now looked as if it never had. She looked like Holly but any sign of life that had been there was now gone, and her face was gaunt.

Tears welded up in Mattie's eyes as she tried to focus on her breathing to remain calm. Morton only stared, no emotion showing on his face as he looked at his daughter. Holly, dressed in a luxurious red dress, looked like she belonged at a party back in New York City. This type of clothing was nothing like what Holly had worn back in Kansas.

"This is her." Morton said looking over at the doctor. The Doctor only nodded at Morton's identification.

"How did she die?" Mattie wiped her tears with a handkerchief.

The doctor cleared his throat. "She was found in her room by one of her girls early in the morning. From what I was able to gather, she seemed to have overdosed on laudanum."

"What do you mean one of *her* girls?" Morton asked dryly. "I also do not approve of the type of dress she is wearing."

Todlen cleared his throat and thought for a moment. "Sir, I mean no disrespect, but what exactly did Miss Holly tell you all she was doing here in Leadville?"

"She had communications with my other daughter here. Seems she had taken work as a seamstress."

"I see." The doctor said as he walked over to the window, overlooking the street.

"Well, what are you getting at? Come on, man, out with it," Morton said, his loud preacher voice starting to take hold.

Todlen turned to face both Mattie and Morton and let out a gentle sigh. "This might come as bit of a shock to the both of you, but Miss Holly was mistress of one of the pleasure houses here in Leadville."

Mattie blinked, not believing what she was hearing and from the loud boom in her father's voice, it was evident neither could he. Morton yelled at the doctor and accused him of lying as he turned back towards the coffin, disgust scratched across his face.

"Sir, I understand the news that you already have been dealing with is of a heavy sort. But Miss Holly *did* partake in that line of work. However, she ran her house very efficiently and cared for all her girls well."

Realization set in and from the problems Morton had had with Holly at a younger age, he seemed to feel what the doctor was saying was true. He stared at the face of his daughter and the repulsion he felt inside, made it to his words. "This *whore* is *not* my daughter!"

And with that, he turned and stormed out of the building.

Mattie's tears ran down her cheeks as she was still very taken aback by the doctor's revelation. The front door slamming behind her father made her snap out of her thoughts and turning she followed him out.

"Father where are you going?" She yelled as he stormed down the boardwalk, bumping into anyone that did not get out of his way.

Picking up her skirt, she tried to run after him. With recent summer rains, the boardwalk was slick, and her foot slipped, throwing her off balance. Trying to grab the side of a building, she slumped down to her knees. Crying out again to her father, the only response was a hand wave of dismissal from him as he disappeared into the crowd of people. Mattie wrapped her arms around herself and cried.

THE FIRST SALOON that Dawson Jones saw was going to be the place he stopped to wet his whistle. The call of whiskey was strong and the Silver Dollar Saloon would be the lucky place he stopped at.

"All right Sandy." Dawson said, looking his mule in the eye. "You stay here and guard what supplies we have left. And don't get any ideas of going off to find some grub. You will get your food soon enough but since it is mostly your fault for dropping our whiskey stash on those rocks, the priority is me getting a drink." And with that Dawson gently patted the mule on the nose and tied the reins to the hitching post.

Taking a deep inhale of the evening air, Dawson slapped his thigh in excitement while letting out a loud yeehaw. From there he made his way into the Silver Dollar Saloon.

The last two months, Dawson had been high up in the mountains, looking for the vein of silver that was going to make him rich. Not only did he not find anything that would improve his wealth class but had also lost all the whiskey during the first month. The whiskey had been tucked away in the pack on Sandy but had fallen off after she had tripped slightly on some rocks. The bottles broke on the rocks, spilling brown liquid all over the ground. Dawson tried his best to keep on but after the second month of no whiskey and not finding his wealth, he decided it was time to head back to Leadville and restock some liquid motivation.

His intention was two drinks but with a couple of his friends also found in the saloon, Dawson was easily convinced to have two more. With a belly full of firewater and conversation he made his way back to the hitching post that he swore he had tied Sandy to. To his surprise, the mule was gone and knowing Sandy's personality, theft was probably not the cause of their sudden disappearance.

Standing outside the livery doors, the proprietor watched Dawson make his way towards him. "Sandy seemed to be impatient for some oats and checked herself in for the night." The man said.

"That stubborn mule has got a mind of her own. She doesn't listen to a damned thing I say George." Dawson said shaking the man's hand.

After haggling over a price for Sandy, Dawson left the livery and was now in search of his own place to find something to eat. He would make his way back to the livery stable later on to sleep in the stall next to Sandy. No need wasting money on a hotel when a bed of straw would suffice just as well.

Walking down Harrison Avenue, a hotel that had a café sign attached to the side of the building caught his eye. Dusting off his clothes for any trail dust that might be still lingering, he made his way into the café. Set up with empty tables and checkered tablecloths, the supper rush seemed over. Removing his hat, Dawson tossed it on the table and sat down as a man came over and took his order of steak, eggs and biscuits. The food came and Dawson dived into his plate and kept the waiter busy bringing him refills of hot, black coffee. The waiter eventually decided to leave a full pot on the table for him.

After the food settled in his belly, Dawson pushed back from the table and let out a happy sigh and paid his bill. Getting up from the table, he made his way to the hotel lobby, stopping to stoke and light his pipe. There was nothing quite like a good hot meal and smoke to him.

A muffled cry came from his right, and he turned to see a woman sitting on a couch up against the window of the lobby. She was wearing a black dress and was holding a handkerchief to her nose. Dawson could tell she had been crying for some time as her eyes were bloodshot and her cheeks puffy. Removing his hat, he walked over to her. "Begging your pardon ma'am, but is everything all right?" Knowing that was a stupid question because a blind man could see that she was not all right.

She glanced up with the deepest blue eyes that Dawson had ever seen. "I am sorry, I am making too much noise."

"Not at all ma'am. I just wanted to make sure you were okay."

She wiped her eyes and adjusted how she was sitting. "I am fine, thank you."

Nodding his head, Dawson turned to walk out the door. Stopping, he turned back. "I am sorry to bother you again ma'am, but do I know you by chance?" He could have sworn that he knew this woman.

"I do not believe so, sir. I have only been in town for a couple days. I am here to—to bury my sister." She said as tears threatened to well up again.

"I am sorry to hear that ma'am." He said, feeling the sorrow he had felt years ago when he buried his own sister. He motioned with his hand to the chair near the couch. "Would you mind if I sat down?"

"Please do but I am not sure I will be much company." She said with a slight smile. "My name is Mattie." She extended her hand and he shook it gently and sat down across from her.

"Pleased to meet you, ma'am. Folks around here call me Dawson."

He studied his pipe briefly. "Did your sister live here in town?"

A sad smile came across her face as she stared out the window. "Yes, she did. She would write to me about this place and how she loved it so. The mountains, the trees, and sunsets." After a moment of reflection, she looked up at Dawson. "Did you know of a Holly Greyson?"

Now Dawson knew why he thought he knew this woman. She resembled Madam Holly of the Mountain Rose almost exactly—even though Mattie had darker hair and a deeper set of blue eyes. With the sad realization of Holly's passing, Dawson looked down at his boots. "I am sorry to hear that she is no longer with us ma'am."

Mattie saw a wave of sadness in his eyes and the almost hidden frown that curved the sides of his mouth beneath his beard. "Did you know her well?"

Blinking his eyes a couple times he said. "I would like to think I did. I have been to her place many times." His face took on a sudden surprised look of panic in realizing what those words might mean to a lady. Fearing he might have overstepped, he quickly fumbled a clearing of his throat. "What I mean is, Miss Holly would sing at her place when the piano player was not too drunk to play, and I always loved to hear her sing."

"She *did* have a lovely voice. She used to sing in our father's church." Mattie said, remembering life with Holly back in Kansas. Her eyes, however, turned emotionless and cold. "No need to hide what my sister was, though Mister Dawson. I have learned quite a bit about my sister over the last couple days. Have even been privy to some of the opinions from the women of this town." Anger took hold of the pretty blue eyes. "Our own father who I came out here with, left Holly at the undertaker's. Claiming that the whore who was in that box was not his daughter" Resentment heavily stained on her words.

Even though she tried to convince her father they needed to take care of Holly's remains and have a funeral for her, he would not be swayed and left on the afternoon train the day before. He had told her to get on the train with him so they could return home but she could not budge from the station platform. Through tears she had watched the train pull away with her father giving another one of his dismissive hand gestures to then turn into the train car.

Knowing how townsfolk could spit judgement from their mouths when it came to things that were preached against heavily on Sundays, Dawson nodded his head slowly. "And what do you think of your sister?"

She shrugged. "I do not know what to think anymore. I knew my sister well in Kansas until our father ran her out for reasons I never understood. We kept in touch and she would write about her life here in the mountains as a seamstress." Looking down at her handkerchief, she seemed to be lost in thought. "Obviously, that was not true, so I wonder if I knew my sister at all." Mattie's eyes seemed like they could tear up again but this time they did not. "She was always so caring to others and was my best friend. I do not know how she could sink so low out here."

He knew of how hard things could be for men in this country, let alone for a woman. The chances were better going up against a grizzly with only an Arkansas toothpick than for a woman to survive out here on her own. He had known many women who had found regular work and still had to scrape everything together to just survive.

"Not to pry into something that is not my business, ma'am." Dawson started but Mattie stopped him. "Please, just call me Mattie. And I would appreciate your insight Mister Dawson."

"Okay, Mattie as long as you just call me Dawson." He replied with a smile, and she nodded in agreement.

"In this life, we play the cards we are dealt. There might be sometimes you can draw another card to try and help your chances but most of the time you just have to play all the way to the laydown. In that you might win or lose." Dawson took a puff on his pipe. "Sometimes even in winning, it does not mean that you had a good hand, it just meant you did your best and did not fold."

"Your sister was an amazing woman. There may be thoughts and concerns about the profession she had chosen for herself but that care for people you mentioned never stopped." Dawson took another puff from his pipe and let the smoke drift from his nostrils. "The big fire a few years back was a doozy and Holly was out in front helping carry buckets of water to put out the flame. Then, covered in soot and ash, she was helping take care of the injured." He stopped and began to refill his pipe. "You don't mind if I keep smoking?" Mattie said that she didn't and that it reminded her of her grandfather when she was very young.

Once his pipe was lit, Dawson continued. "When the terrible fever came through camp, she turned her place into one of the infirmaries and nursed many of us old boys back to health, including yours truly."

Mattie continued to speak to Dawson until she decided to call it a night. He told her that he was glad to have met her and that he would be pulling out in the morning. She bid him farewell and hoped that he would find what he was looking for. On her way up the stairs, the hotel clerk told her that Dr. Todlen left her a package earlier that day. Taking it upstairs, she left it on the small vanity in the corner of the room.

THE LOUD AND rambunctious crowd made their way through the streets going from saloons, restaurants, and houses of ill repute. Mud and the time of day be damned. Mattie lay in her bed at the hotel staring at the ceiling, lost in thought as sleep would not come to her. Thinking about the evening, her time with Dawson had been the most positive thing she had experienced in a long time. Seeming like a rough mountain man, which he did dress and talk the part, he did have a soft spot that seemed to come out the more they spoke to each other.

The hours ticked by, and Mattie could not help but wonder how Holly could not tell her the way her life had turned out. A cold thought of regret quickly washed over her at the thought that Holly felt ashamed or scared to tell her or that she would have the same views as their father. Mattie asked Holly in her letters what had happened between her and father and the letters she received seemed to skip the subject all together, so Mattie quit asking. She also knew there was no chance that Morton would tell her what had happened.

Hearing the voices of Holly, her father, and even Dawson play though her mind, Mattie finally sat up and shook her head. Getting up from the bed, she walked over to the vanity and picked up the package from Todlen. A letter was attached with her name on it and a small message stating that these were some of the items that were Holly's. A woman who worked for Holly had brought them to the doctor earlier that day.

Opening the package, she pulled out a hair pin with a beautiful design of flowers on it. Mattie had a matching one that was now on the nightstand when she had let down her hair for the night. Both girls had been given these by their mother, a year before she had died.

There was a hairbrush, some tin pictures, and some letters. In the message the doctor said she could pick up the other items of Holly's from the Mountain Rose at her convenience. She opened a letter that was addressed to her and looking at the date, it was from almost three years ago but had never been sent. Mattie unfolded the old letter and reading it, the words seemed as if they could be her sister talking to her now even though they had been written years before.

Tears filled Mattie's eyes learning the truth behind her father running Holly out onto the prairie. Being with child from one of the local farm hands, her father saw no mercy and cast her out. She went to the man who she had fallen in love with and whose child she was carrying only to have him deny it was his and sent her on her way. With nowhere to go, Holly made it to Denver, Colorado where she ended up having a little baby girl named Pearl. Finding work was hard so Holly went to work for Madame Frolly in a brothel rather than letting Pearl and herself starve. She was able to keep Pearl at the house where she worked and some of the other women who worked there would help watch the baby. A short time later, Madame Frolly decided to move her girls up to Leadville. Over the next couple years, Holly had gained favor with Madame Frolly and when the madame had died suddenly, she left everything to Holly.

Holly did not want to cast out the women she was working with into the snow, so she continued the business. Coming into a fair share of money, she took great care of the women who worked for her and tried to do right by them as best she could.

Not long after taking over the Mountain Rose, Pearl died of Scarlet

Fever. That was near the end of the letter, but it wrapped up saying that Holly was still suffering after losing Pearl but trying to push on with her new role. She then apologized for not telling Mattie the truth sooner and that she would have been a loving aunt to Pearl.

Mattie held the letter to her chest and sobbed. She had had a niece and Holly had been sent out into cold by both her father and the man she loved to figure it out on her own. How hard that must have been and Mattie could only feel sorrow that she could have helped her sister if she had known the truth. Mattie wrote to Holly about visiting her, but Holly would say it was not a good time and that they would be able to soon.

With Holly now gone, Mattie was glad Pearl had her mommy with her again. And the thought of both being with Mattie's mother in heaven gave her the sense of peace that she had been looking for.

Maybe what Dawson said about having to do the best we can with what we have was true. It now seemed to her, Holly did the best with what life had thrown at her and had even done more than just survive.

After reading the letter, Mattie had finally found sleep and waking up that next morning, felt more refreshed than she had been in a long time. After breakfast, she set up arrangements for Holly's funeral with the undertaker and learned that Holly bought the plot next to Pearl for herself so she could be buried next to her daughter.

LATER THAT EVENING, Mattie made her way down the stairs for supper to find Dawson waiting for her. "Dawson. I expected you to be gone this morning." She said with a little surprise in her voice.

"Yes, ma'am—I mean *Mattie.*" He scratched at his beard. "I was up late thinking and did not get going as early as I thought I would."

"Seems neither of us got much sleep last night." Mattie smiled.

"I heard that you're going to have a service tomorrow for Holly?"

"Yes. I learned that she had a daughter who is buried in the Evergreen Cemetery. She will be laid next to her."

"Miss Holly never said anything about losing a child. Seems she played life close to the chest."

"I believe my sister had enormous hurts inside that she kept to herself." Mattie said with a small sigh. "Doctor Todlen mentioned that Holly was having some dark days and was coaxing it with laudanum from one of the women who worked for her. It looks as if the laudanum got the best of her" Mattie wiped a tear away.

"This all must be very hard on you, Mattie." Dawson said and took both of Mattie's hands into his own. "Would you indulge me to show you something briefly? It will require stepping foot into a saloon, but I think you will find it worthwhile. And we will only be in there a few minutes."

A week ago, Mattie might have been offended but after her most recent experiences and the trust she had in Dawson, she agreed. They both walked down to the Silver Dollar Saloon where a wild crowd was celebrating the night away.

Mattie stood inside, off from the front door as Dawson tried yelling to get the crowd's attention, to no avail. He finally stood up on a table and pulling his old Navy Colt from his belt, fired a round into the ceiling.

"Howdy, boys!" He yelled as the crowd now turned their full attention to him.

Almost in unison the crowd responded back with "Howdy, Daws!"

"Boys, this fine lady by the door is the sister of the late great Madam Holly!" As Dawson spoke, the men all slowly removed their hats. "She's putting together a funeral service for tomorrow and I know how much Miss Holly meant to all of you as she did me." Dawson went on how Holly had cared for them and nursed a lot of them back to health. "Would you all show Miss Mattie Greyson how much her sister meant to you by showing up tomorrow?" The room cheered and hats were thrown into the air. Mattie couldn't help but feel the love swell in the room for her sister.

A very thin man with a southern accent, walked up to Mattie to offer his hand as he introduced himself as John Holliday. He told her how special a woman Holly was and how sorry he was for her loss. "Thank you, Mister Holliday."

He kissed the top of her hand. "Please, call me Doc." With a wink, he turned across the room, and began coughing violently. Stopping, he downed the whiskey in the glass that he held.

THE FOLLOWING DAY, Leadville held the biggest funeral in its short history, all in honor of Holly Greyson. The long funeral procession followed the hearse from town to the Evergreen Cemetery while a band played music for the journey. The crowd was so large at the grave site, the pastor giving the service had to yell. Mattie Greyson stood next to the grave with Dawson Jones by her side. Pearl Greyson's marker was a small wooden cross that read *Beloved Child Now With The Lord.* Mattie laid fresh flowers on the grave and while everyone sang "Amazing Grace," she reached over and took hold of Dawson's hand. He gently took it into his and looked over into her blue eyes and smiled, a small tear streaming down his cheek.

—Since he was a small child, Ben Bailey has been in love with Westerns. He was born and raised in Colorado and in 3rd grade fell in love with the history of the American west. He likes to travel to different historical sites and imagine the brave men and women from all walks of life, who braved the frontier.

CRY, "INDIANS!"

ANTHONY WOOD

A YOUNG COW puncher raced to the front of the slow moving herd of cattle in the fury of a twister. Jake Baker drew up in a skidding stop and pulled down his bandana. He coughed and spat, wiping the grime from his eyes.

"Indians, Boss! In those hills over there! I saw them!"

Boss Jack Ray squinted in the direction the boy pointed. He waved over two other hands and yelled, "Go check that draw to the west." Boss pointed his thumb at Jake. "The boy thinks he's seen Injuns." He turned to Jake and snidely said, "Once again."

Jake snickered to himself and turned to go with the two hands trotting toward the hills.

Boss barked, "Oh, heck no. Not you, Jake. They'll handle it. Especially since they ain't gonna find nobody there no ways."

Jake covered his mouth to hide a grin. He changed the subject. "Trail dust is really hard to eat riding in the unhealthy position of drag when you do not have even a drop of water left in your canteen with which to wash it down, boss."

Boss glared and snarled, "Yeah, it is, when the man, or should I say, the boy, who was s'pposed to fill everybody's canteen this mornin' thought it was so funny to hang 'em on the men's saddles with only two swallers each. Yeah, dust makes a mighty dry meal that's hard to choke down without water." Boss slaps his knee. "Dang, Jake, men been havin' to leave the herd to get water all day long. It's slowed us down and I ain't havin' it. You get your butt back there on drag like I told you and stay there. I ain't payin' you to complain or play tricks. I'm payin' you to help me drive these critters to Abilene, no more and no less."

Jake cried out like a little boy afraid of his own shadow, "But there was something back there, Boss. I swear I saw Indians. Did you understand me correctly?"

"Yeah, I heard you callin'. We all did. But we're tired of runnin' after mirages and such."

"But I saw those Indians hiding in the draw we just passed. But you do not—"

Boss reined up short. "Don't *what,* boy? Believe you? Why should I?"

"You should trust me when I call, Boss, and come as quickly as you—"

Boss removed his hat to swat Jake. "Now you're gonna try and tell me how to run my own outfit?"

Jake ducked his head down so the brim of his hat covered his smiling eyes. "No, sir, I am not."

"You've been jumpy as a two dollar whore sittin' on the front row bench in a holy-roller revival service at altar call since your pa got snake bit last year. Get it in that thick head of yorn, son, there ain't a rattler, ruffian, or an Injun behind every bush you ride by. You're gonna have to settle yourself down and stop all this play actin'. Toughen up and start actin' like a man."

"I'm trying, Boss. I really do see things, but when you and the men get there, they seem to have all disappeared."

"And this makes how times we done raced off chasin' after some Injun or outlaw you swore you've seen, only to find there ain't nothin' but tumbleweeds, jackrabbits, or just some swayin' willer trees when we get there?" Boss barks, "Tell me!"

Jake, trying not to laugh, coughed in order to cover up his uncontrollable outburst.

"I've had enough of your ignert and stupid ways. Now git on back there where you're s'pposed to be or I'll take a short rope to your backside like your pa should have, God rest his soul."

Jake reined his mount around and galloped back to end of the line, disappearing into a sea of dust, but laughing. He pulled up behind the last steer and slowed to a walk. He rubbed his horse's neck, contemplating his next deception.

"Yeah old boy, we're having a good time playing around with the old man and the boys. Call me stupid? We'll see who the stupid ones are, just you wait and see."

JAKE BAKER WAS a silly boy. His father died miserably last year when the biggest rattler anybody had ever seen bit him while he was cooking up grub for the men who were branding calves near the chuck wagon. What Boss didn't know was that Jake had put cow chips in the beans when his pa wasn't looking, thinking it would be the joke of the century. At least that's what he thought, until his pa tasted the beans and nearly puked scraping the rancid slop out of his mouth with his bandana.

"I'll get you for this, Jake, you just wait," Jake's father yelled as he rushed down to the creek to wash his mouth out. That's when the rattler got him, square on the neck when he knelt down to scoop up some water. He screamed in agony and Jake called the other drovers to come quick. By the time they got to him, the poison had already reached his heart and he was convulsing. Jake slinked back to the chuck wagon to get rid of the evidence—fouled beans for a joke gone sour.

Jake laughed to himself and said as he took the bean pot into the bushes, "That's what you get for thinking I'm so stupid, Pa. I'm not. I just like to have a little fun, as long as it's not at my expense."

Boss Jack Ray slipped up behind Jake as he was dumping out the pot of beans.

"What're you doin', boy? Ain't you got no sense? No feelin'? You're pa just died and you're over here dumpin' out our supper? What's gotten into you, son?"

Jake had to think fast. So he lied. "I don't know. I guess I didn't want anyone eating the last meal Pa cooked. I guess I lost my head," Jake whined, but secretly snickering to himself.

"Well, son, I know you're upset, but… well… I guess I don't have to understand." Boss took off his hat and scratched his head. "Get yourself together. We're buryin' your father before sundown." Boss Jack Ray walked away, shaking his head. "That boy ain't right in the head. I don't know what I'm gonna…."

Jake whispered as Boss Jack Ray wandered back over where his father lay stretched out on a plank, "And good riddance to you, too, old man. And the rest of you? You're the stupid ones. I'm smarter than all of you put together. I'm going show you how clever I am."

His face got hot. His hands started shaking. Jake growled, "Call me crazy, will you?"

He slung the bean pot straight into the canvas covering the chuck wagon. The group of cowboys turned with pistols drawn.

Boss Jack Ray patted the air with his hands. "It's all right, boys. He's upset that his pa just died." Boss took another look at Jake, and then whispered to the others, "There's somethin' really wrong with that boy. Y'all keep an eye out." Boss turned back around and smiled at Jake like he'd said nothing.

Jake hissed under his breath, "You think I don't know, old man, what you and the rest of your imbeciles think of me. You want to talk about me behind my back? All right, then. Go ahead. I'll get you dunces back. All of you. Watch what I'm telling you. I'm going to wear all of you out making you think there's trouble on every turn. You'll wish you'd never talked down to Jake Baker. No sir, you will soon regret you ever heard the name Jake Baker."

And they buried Jake Baker's father down by the creek. He stood off at a distance, grinning.

Time for the big round up and the drive to Abilene came early that year. Boss Jack Ray had kept young Jake on the payroll because he had respect for his dead father and to help his mother who struggled to make ends meet. Jake had nowhere else to go and Boss knew it. Because he was known to be a troublemaker, no one would hire him on, and Boss's cowhands constantly complained about the boy's incessant pranking. He'd done everything he could think of to cause them grief. They'd done everything they knew to do to settle him down, shy of taking a red hot JR Ranch branding iron to his behind. Nothing worked—neither their efforts help knock some sense into his head nor their complaining to Boss.

Boss's foreman, Riley, finally asked, "Why are you keepin' that boy on? He ain't nothin' but trouble all the time."

"I know, but that boy's got some real smarts. He's been to school and knows his numbers. You hear him talk, don't you? Near perfect English if I ever heard it. He's either a genius or a full-fledged idiot. I ain't quite figured out which. But his poor Ma won't make it through the winter without Jake's pay, so I keep him on to help her out." Boss scratched the back of his neck. "I'm hopin' he'll grow up some workin' with us. I thought a lot of his pa and I want help Jake make somethin' of himself. Problem is I don't know how much longer I can take his shenanigans."

Riley kicked the dirt, and spat his tobacco to the side. "Boss, me and the boys done 'bout had all we can stand of his foolishness. Genius or no genius, he's becomin' downright criminal, if you ask me. I'm tellin' you here and now, somebody's fixin' to get hurt. We never know what that kid's gonna do next. None of us feel like we can relax enough to eat our grub in peace, hit the bushes when nature calls, or even sleep good at night. I'm afeared somebody's gonna lose their temper and—"

"Don't you do anythin' to hurt him, you hear? And that goes for the rest of the boys, too. This will take care of itself. Just give it a little time. I don't know how, but watch what I tell you."

THE TWO COWPUNCHERS trotted back to where Boss sat on his horse overlooking the herd from a hilltop. Once again, they found no Indians. It was just a herd of deer drifting through the brush. Jake could see from his position at drag through the dust the two men shaking their heads, then Boss slamming his hat on his thigh. Jake just laughed and straightened his bandana to look like the outlaws he'd read about in the dime novels.

He patted his mount's neck. "This is getting better by the minute, old boy."

They made good time that day. Water was near and the cattle could smell it. The herd picked the pace and the cowboys started bunching them together for the river crossing. And of course, Jake had disappeared again.

Boss stood up in his saddle to check the end of the herd. He shielded his eyes from the sun, looking in every direction. He asked Riley, "Where is that crazy boy?"

Riley shook his head. "Hell if I know, Boss. Prolly swimmin' in the river up ahead."

Boss sat back down in his saddle and slapped his saddle horn, and yelled, "Dang it! Call me a preacher but hear me cuss, I'm done with that knot head. We've already lost a dozen head of cattle wastin' time with that boy's mischief."

Riley stood up in his saddle, cupping his ears. "Wait! Hear that? Up there at the river. Somebody's hollerin' and cryin' out somethin' about Injuns! I best get on up there to see if—"

Boss stuck his hand out across the foreman's chest. "Nope, not this time. He can have his stupid fun without us."

"But Boss, what if—"

"That's just too damn bad. He's earned this one. I ain't sendin' nobody out after him. He'll come around when it's bean time."

The cattle herd started trotting toward the river ready for a drink and to cool off.

Boss gently prodded his mount. "Guess we better get on up there and find a place to water the herd and cross the stream."

They gasped as they rode up to edge of a small bluff overlooking the shallow river.

There lay Jake at edge of the sandy river bank, scalped, with two arrows stuck in his chest.

—Anthony grew up in historic Natchez, Mississippi, fueling a life-long love of history. Not long after high school, he lived and worked in Alaska for several years. He returned to the South and ministered for nearly three decades among

the poor, homeless, and incarcerated before retiring to become a full-time author. His first novel, the critically-acclaimed Civil War epic White & Black, *hit the shelves in 2021. Five sequels have followed, with another scheduled for 2024. His short story, "Not So Long in the Tooth" won a Will Rogers Medallion Award. Anthony is the 2024 Arkansas Writers' Hall of Fame inductee. When not writing, Anthony enjoys roaming and researching historical sites, camping and kayaking on the Mississippi River, and being with family . Anthony and his wife, Lisa, live in Conway, Arkansas.*

One of Geronimo's Braves by Henry Farny

HAT CREEK

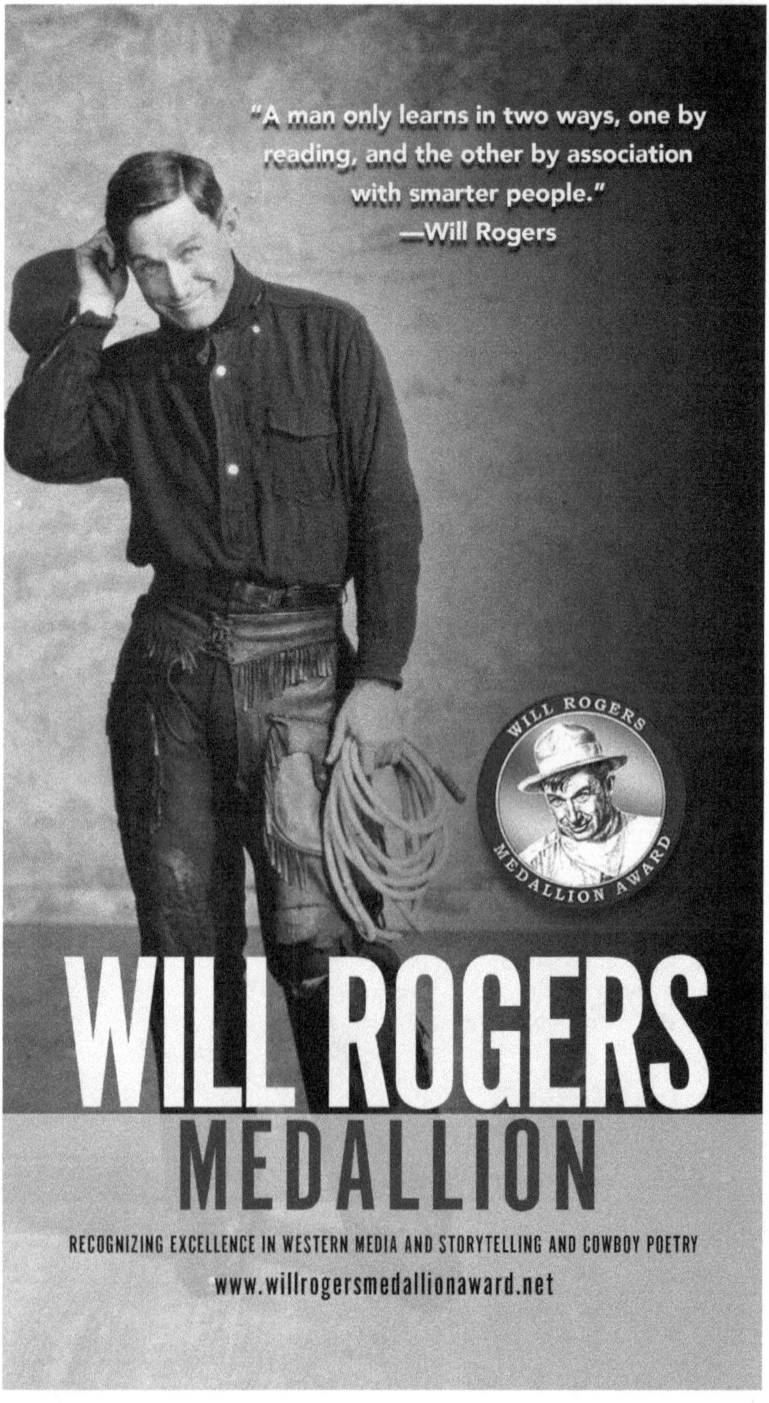
"A man only learns in two ways, one by reading, and the other by association with smarter people."
—Will Rogers
WILL ROGERS MEDALLION AWARD
WILL ROGERS
MEDALLION
RECOGNIZING EXCELLENCE IN WESTERN MEDIA AND STORYTELLING AND COWBOY POETRY
www.willrogersmedallionaward.net

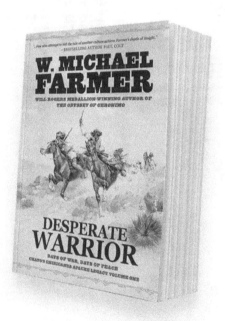

The Perfect Combination.
Big Nose Kate Whiskey & According to Kate:
The Legendary Life of Big Nose Kate, Love of Doc Holliday
BNK
BIG NOSE KATE
ACCORDING TO
KATE
CHRIS ENSS
Visit Big Nose Kate Whiskey at https://bignosekate.co/home to learn about the brave and adventurous blend and www.chrisenss.com to learn about the bestselling book dedicated to one of the most infamous Western characters of all time.

NEW YORK TIMES BESTSELLING AUTHOR
REAVIS Z. WORTHAM
"I'll read anything Reavis Z. Wortham writes!"
—MARC CAMERON,
NEW YORK TIMES BESTSELLING AUTHOR
THE CAP WHITLATCH SERIES
THE ONLY SALOON IN TOWN
A CAP WHITLATCH WESTERN
REAVIS WORTH
AVAILABLE 9/24/24
"WORTHAM WRITES WITH PITCH-PERFECT WEST TEXAS FLAVOR." —Lone Star Literary Life
THE JOURNEY SOUTH
A CAP WHITLATCH WESTERN
REAVIS Z. WORTHAM
TWO-TIME WINNER OF THE SPUR AWARD
BARNES & NOBLE
kobo

Printed in the USA
CPSIA information can be obtained
at www.ICGtesting.com
LVHW041615300824
789714LV00001B/211

9 781633 739628